TABLE OF CONTENTS

Disclaimer

This is a work of historical fiction. While it incorporates references to actual historical figures, places, events, and cultural elements, the story itself is a product of the author's imagination. Any dialogue, thoughts, actions, or characterizations attributed to real historical individuals are fictionalized and should not be interpreted as factual accounts. Certain names, locations, and incidents have been used fictitiously or altered for dramatic purposes. Any resemblance to actual persons, living or deceased, beyond well-known historical figures, is purely coincidental. The author has made reasonable efforts to ensure historical accuracy where appropriate, but liberties have been taken to create a compelling narrative. This book should not be read as a definitive history or biography.

CHAPTER 1: REFLECTIONS OF A CULTURAL MELANGE

Ishiki Nakamura stood at the entrance of Nakamozu Station, a welcoming blend of modernity and tradition, where the cacophony of commuters fused with the aromas of nearby shops. The flickering lights of festive decorations danced above him, casting a supportive glow on the throngs of people bustling in and out. He adjusted the strap of his small backpack, running a hand through his casually styled short black hair, spotting a familiar figure weaving through the crowd: Vivian 'Bibian' Moon, a bright spot amidst the sea of winter coats.

"Bibian!" he called, raising a hand and trying to extricate himself from the press of locals hurrying past. Her bright colors stood out like a beacon, gathering smiles from others around. She wove through the throngs with the ease of a fish navigating water, her petite frame somehow leaving space for her vivacious spirit even in the densest crowds.

"Hey, Ishiki!" Bibian's cheerful voice rang out. She promptly deposited her colorful backpack onto her shoulder with a slight bounce, grinning from ear to ear. "Look at this!" She produced a box from her bag, showcasing a decorated Christmas cake, sparkling with icing and adorned with little reindeer figures. "I found it at the local bakery. It smells amazing!"

Ishiki's eyes widened in delight. "That looks incredible! Yuki will love this. You know how much she enjoys exploring seasonal pastries." He loved the way Bibian found joy in even the smallest details, drawing attention to something as ordinary as a cake and transforming it into an unforgettable experience.

"Yuki and Akira are meeting us at the karaoke box later, right?" Bibian bounced on the balls of her feet, her enthusiasm palpable. The prospect of friends, laughter, and music filled her with an infectious energy.

"Yes! They've been looking forward to it all week. I think Akira has some new songs lined up, too." Ishiki grinned, amused by the way Bibian's excitement made him feel particularly nostalgic about their past karaoke adventures.

As they stepped into the cozy warmth of the karaoke establishment, colors flickered like a vibrant rainbow. Walls were decorated with photos of famous artists and the latest hits, illuminated by neon lights that pulsed softly with the beat of songs vibrating through the air. They approached the front desk, exchanging friendly banter with the staff, gesturing playfully with their fingers to signal how many hours they planned to stay. The karaoke box itself was small, just enough to do what they loved most—sing, laugh, and truly escape.

With their room secured, Bibian pulled out her phone, scrolling through the extensive song list displayed there. "What about starting with some classic Japanese ballads?" she suggested, eyes sparkling. "I'm eager to sing something traditional."

Ishiki chuckled, "I should have guessed you'd go for that. Let's make it a mix tonight —Christmas songs and Japanese classics can blend beautifully!"

They took their places in the soundproof room, adorning themselves with the soft glow of the lights that flickered with a gentle pulse. Ishiki held the microphone, his fingers tapping lightly against its cool metal surface.

"I'll start with this one," Ishiki said, throwing a teasing smile at Bibian. "Let me show you the depth of my 'Japanese soul'!"

The first few notes filled the room, and Ishiki began to sing an old ballad that echoed with sentimental tones. Bibian watched him, her wide eyes, and soft laughter adding to the atmosphere. The simplicity of sharing a song created a space where culture met companionship, where every lyric and note blended with the joy of their differences.

As Ishiki sang, he lost himself in the melody, reflecting on how the layers of his world had changed significantly since meeting Bibian. His thoughts wandered back to their first days together—nervous exchanges, attempts to explain the nuances of Japanese traditions, and how she would light up whenever she talked about Taiwan's festivals. It had caused him to see his own culture through new eyes, revealing beauty hidden in the ordinary.

When they finished up that song, Bibian leapt up, arms waving. "I loved that! You should try a duet with me next!" She sang out, before diving into a playful rendition of a contemporary pop song, her petite frame embodying every vibrant inflection of her lively performance.

After a few rounds of songs, the door swung open, and Akira Yamamoto stepped in, jogging his way inside with a smile. "Did I miss anything?" he joked, his tall form eclipsing the doorway. Dressed smartly in a blazer over a simple shirt, he radiated a calm confidence that always grounded their exuberance.

"Just our initial warm-up!" Ishiki replied, gesturing for Akira to join them. "Bibian has been waiting to unleash some new talent!"

"Ready to be amazed," Akira quipped, reaching for the microphone. They continued cycling through songs, laughing at off-key notes, occasionally breaking out into spontaneous dance moves despite the limited space.

Yuki Tanaka arrived, her shoulder-length brown hair freshly tucked into a bun, looking cute in a pastel sweater. With an excited wave, she quickly set down her bags and joined the fray. "I brought some snacks for us!" she exclaimed, rummaging through her backpack. "And I also prepared an epic playlist—perfect songs from all our cultures!"

As the karaoke battle continued, Yuki's laughter melded with Bibian's enthusiastic shouts, creating a delightful harmony that filled the room with warmth. That night highlighted distinct flavors, from festive classics to modern hits. It became a celebration of their diverse backgrounds, sampling life's sweet dishes like a five-course meal.

"Hey, can we take a break?" Ishiki suggested after an hour of belting their hearts out. He reached for the Christmas cake Bibian had brought, the icing reflecting the fantastic neon lights around them.

"Good idea! Dancing burns a lot of energy," Bibian replied playfully.

They huddled around the small table filled with treats, the cake featuring layers of vanilla and strawberry, glistening under the ambient lights. Ishiki cut generous slices with Yuki's help, and they all gathered, eager to delve into the delicious creation.

"This cake is delightful! It makes me feel like I'm celebrating two cultures at once," Bibian declared, her infectious energy making the atmosphere even warmer. Ishiki observed how she navigated their diverse traditions effortlessly, embodying the spirit of Christmas through her genuine appreciation.

"Do you guys have traditional Christmas cakes in Taiwan?" Yuki asked, genuinely curious.

Bibian nodded, her smile unwavering. "Yes, we have all kinds of cakes, but we also enjoy egg tarts and sweet meats during the celebrations. I've been dying to introduce you to them, so we should plan a night together!"

The friends exchanged excited chatter about the blend of culinary experiences they could bring to the table, each of them contributing their cultural heritages to the feast.

"I love the idea! You know, we could combine some of our recipes for Christmas next year," Akira mused, pulling out his phone and tapping it enthusiastically. "Imagine a fusion feast! Sugary sweet Taiwanese pastries alongside our beloved Christmas cakes."

"Count me in for that!" Ishiki exclaimed, glancing around the room at his friends. With every song, every shared laugh, and every delightful conversation, a tapestry of traditions and cherished memories was being woven together.

Bibian's eyes sparkled. "And we can end with a karaoke performance, of course! Who doesn't want to serenade their guests?"

With enthusiasm, they dove back into their karaoke chorus, but the cake slowly disappeared, making way for shared stories, laughter, and a camaraderie that thrived on their cultural similarities and differences.

As the night wound down, Bibian sat back, a satisfied grin plastered on her face. "What a perfect way to prepare for Christmas! I love how we're making our traditions mesh."

Ishiki smiled, the warmth from the cake and the sounds of their voices lingering in the air. "It's about creating new traditions, right? Celebrating all this together allows our cultures to blend beautifully."

As the last notes of a Christmas ballad floated through the room, Ishiki felt the weight of his thoughts dissolve into laughter and song. The night transformed into a beautiful melange of his upbringing, Bibian's vibrant experiences, and his friends' nurturing spirits. It was a reminder of the season's essence—togetherness, joy, and the unity that comes from diving into one another's cultures.

Leaving the karaoke box that night, the sidewalks of Nakamozu Station sparkled with the remnants of the holiday lights, mirroring their hearts full of shared experiences. Ishiki felt optimistic about what lay ahead, knowing that time could only bring more stories—more carols sung, more memories made, and a deeper blending of their worlds.

CHAPTER 2: RAMEN AND REMINISCENCE

The soft glow of Nakamozu Station released a sigh of warmth as Ishiki and Bibian stepped back into the bustling atmosphere late that night. Carrying the remnants of their karaoke session—the contagious laughter and shared songs—inside, they were both feeling the gentle embrace of the winter air that contrasted sharply with the heartwarming feelings they had cultivated during the evening. Bibian, still buzzing from the excitement, clapped her hands together as they made their way to the nearest ramen shop.

"Ishiki, do you think we could grab a late-night bowl before heading back?" Bibian's eyes sparkled with enthusiasm, resembling a child on the brink of a great adventure.

"Absolutely! Nothing beats a steaming bowl of ramen after singing your heart out," he chuckled, recalling the various flavors and combinations he had enjoyed over the years. "Plus, it's perfect for that cold night breeze, isn't it?"

As they walked, Ishiki thought about how food had been a backdrop to many of their cultural exchanges. It was in the ramen shop that they had first connected over their differing taste preferences, and somehow, the warm bowls of noodles in front of them bridged their worlds even further.

The narrow entrance of the ramen shop welcomed them inside, instantly engulfing them in the aromatic symphony of broth, spice, and freshly prepared noodles. The walls, lined with vintage photographs of past culinary masters, echoed tales of long-standing tradition. The small space was crowded, a testament to its popularity, and the laughter and cheers added a lively ambiance.

Bibian eagerly took a seat at the counter, her petite frame barely visible behind a high stack of bowls. "Look at all the varieties of ramen! I can't believe how incredible this place smells!" She leaned closer to the menu, her eyes darting over the enticing descriptions filled with mouth-watering ingredients.

Ishiki watched as she debated between the tonkotsu (pork bone) and shoyu (soy sauce) ramen, her excitement contagious. "You'll have to try the spicy miso ramen one day, too. It has a perfect kick!" he suggested. "But you should stick to the classic for your first time here—especially since we've had all that sweet cake."

Bibian nodded, considering his words seriously, before smiling again. "You're right! It seems fitting to start with something authentic. I'm going to ask the chef for their recommendation."

As she waved over the chef, whose warm presence added to the overall vibe of the shop, Ishiki couldn't help but reminisce about their initial encounters over cultural meals. Their culinary adventures had often turned into history lessons wrapped in flavors. Bibian had schooled him on Taiwanese snacks, while he had introduced her to traditional Japanese dishes. Each meal was a dive into their heritage, but ramen had quickly become a favorite shared experience. It was through ramen that they had first discussed the broader themes of cultural exchange—the narratives that tied people and places together regardless of distance or differences.

When the steaming bowls of ramen arrived, the rich broth swirled with vibrant colors of soft-boiled eggs, green onions, and slices of freshly cooked chashu pork. The sight was almost too beautiful to disturb.

"Wow, it looks even better in person!" Bibian exclaimed, scooping her chopsticks, ready to dive into the deliciousness. "Let's do a toast—with our ramen?"

Ishiki laughed and lifted his bowl slightly, mirroring her actions. "To cultural exchanges, delicious food, and new memories!" They clanked their bowls together before digging in.

From the first slurp, Bibian's face lit up, and a smile erupted like the spring sun breaking through winter clouds. "This is amazing! The flavor is so rich—how do you guys make it taste like love?"

Ishiki chuckled, pleased to see her reaction. "That's the secret ingredient—passion, and a bit of patience. Every bowl carries the heart of the chef, you know?"

"I feel that," Bibian replied, savoring another mouthful. After a brief pause, she leaned back slightly, her expression turning introspective. "I've been thinking about how food tells such a rich story. It's different everywhere, yet it's also so similar in ways. It's comforting."

"Absolutely," Ishiki nodded, passion igniting as he spoke. "Ramen here in Japan carries the spirit of community. It's something you can share with friends, family, or even strangers. It brings everyone together, just like tonight's karaoke. Sharing experiences fosters understanding among different perspectives."

Bibian paused, pondering his words, eyes reflecting the flickering lights of the shop. "I think about that a lot—how we might be from such different cultures, yet when we sit down together, we can share laughter, stories, and traditions. It's like creating a bridge, one bowl of ramen at a time."

Ishiki noticed how she spoke with sincerity, a reminder of why their friendship held significance; it was more than seeking differences, but collaboratively building a tapestry of similarities. He admired her ability to weave in and out of cultural reflections effortlessly, and more importantly, how she encouraged him to see his own culture anew.

"Speaking of bridges, do you have any special holiday traditions in Taiwan?" he asked, genuinely interested, the warmth of the ramen gently soothing the cold creeping in from outside.

"Oh, definitely!" Bibian leaned closer, animated by the topic. "In Taiwan, we have a unique way of celebrating Christmas. Though it's not a traditional holiday, we still celebrate in our way. It's a blend of Western influences and our own customs."

Ishiki leaned in, intrigued. "I'd love to learn about them! What do you typically do?"

She took another sip of her broth, the heat flowing through her until she started reminiscing. "Well, the food is a big part of it! We often prepare winter delicacies—

like candy and pastries, and we have this thing called 'Christmas cake' too, similar to what we had tonight. But there's a twist; it incorporates dried fruits, and we might even add a touch of local teas. Besides that, we decorate with lights and sing songs, often drawing from both Western music and our traditional melodies."

Ishiki could see the narrative playing out in her mind as she recalled each detail, animated by the memories. "That sounds beautiful. I love how you incorporate both aspects! It's like creating a unique culture within a celebration."

"Exactly!" Bibian beamed at his understanding. "And on Christmas Eve, we usually gather around and share stories. It doesn't just focus on gift-giving but also about being together—just like us tonight."

He nodded in agreement, tasting the flavor of connections deepening between their cultures. "That's something I cherish as well in Japan. The spirit of the New Year holds similar meaning—people often gather to share their hopes and dreams through food and celebration. It's a time for reflection and togetherness, where you appreciate those around you."

Their conversation continued through the meal, filled with laughter punctuated by spirited stories, and soon the ramen bowls lay empty before them, reflecting the camaraderie they built. As they finished, Bibian's ponytail bounced with enthusiasm, and she looked at Ishiki with sparkling eyes. "So, how about a small Christmas gathering—the four of us? You, me, Akira, and Yuki. We could share our traditions, blend our favorite dishes, and create new ones!"

Ishiki's heart warmed at the idea. "That sounds incredible! We can finalize the plans over a group video call. Each of us can bring something from our culture, and we can celebrate our unique fusion."

"Perfect!" Bibian's excitement was infectious. "I'll bring some Taiwanese delectables —those egg tarts I mentioned earlier, and let's add some decorations too!"

As they exited the shop, the chilly air biting at their cheeks, Ishiki felt an anticipation stirring within. "I'm looking forward to watching all our traditions blend together."

Walking along the city streets, vibrant lights twinkled above the rhythm of their footsteps, as if the city itself was enveloping them in the holiday spirit. The laughter and chatter of people mingled with the crisp air filled with hints of celebration.

In that moment, Ishiki felt hopeful. It wouldn't just be a mix of foods or songs; it would be a celebration of relationships—the ones they nurtured over a meal, the ones that crossed borders and cultures, and those that endured through stories shared. Each step forward was testimony to their growing friendship.

"Do you think we should find more places like the ramen shop for our gathering?" Bibian asked, glancing over at him, her eyes alight with inspiration.

"Definitely," he said. "Exploring together will keep the spirit of our exchange alive. And speaking of places, we'll have to find the right spot for karaoke… again!"

Her laughter filled the air, mixing with the sounds of the city as they made their way home, each reflection of nostalgia stirring excitement for the new memories they would create. As they walked, the blend of cultures, laughter, and the shared journey brought them closer together, bridging their worlds one experience at a time.

CHAPTER 3: AN UNEXPECTED REUNION

The crisp winter air welcomed Ishiki as he stepped out of his apartment early the next morning, bright sunlight filtering through the trees lining the street. The sounds of Nakamozu Station were already beginning, a swirl of activity that hinted at another busy day. He tightened the drawstrings of his comfortable hoodie, glancing at the calendar on his phone. Only a week remained until Christmas, and thoughts of his upcoming gathering with Bibian, Akira, and Yuki filled him with warmth and excitement. They had spent the last few weeks planning the culinary adventure, each friend bringing components of their culture and heritage into the mix.

Ishiki decided to stop by the local bakery—the quaint shop he had mentioned to Bibian a few days ago, renowned for its seasonal pastries. He imagined the delightful Christmas cakes lined up in the window, enticing pedestrians with their sweet aroma. As the door jingled open, he was greeted by the comforting scent of fresh bread and sugar.

"Good morning, Ishiki!" greeted the baker, an elderly man with flour dusting his apron and a jovial sparkle in his eyes. "What can I get you today?"

"Good morning! I'd like to see the Christmas cakes you mentioned!" Ishiki smiled, eager to explore what the bakery had on offer.

The baker nodded with a knowing chuckle, leading him to the display case where an assortment of cakes sat, adorned with colorful icing and decorative holly. "These are made fresh every day. We have a Japanese-style strawberry shortcake and a rich matcha cream cake this year."

Ishiki's eyes widened in delight. "They all look amazing! I'll take the matcha cream cake and one of the strawberry shortcakes, please." He imagined presenting them during their gathering, a symbol of his culture's culinary joys.

"Excellent choice!" The baker wrapped the cakes carefully before handing them over with a bright smile. "You're in for a treat!"

"Thank you!" Ishiki waved goodbye as he stepped back into the chilly air. The cakes nestled securely in their boxes felt like treasures, ready to add sweetness to the celebration. He paused for a moment, enjoying the bustling energy around him, watching families rush past him to catch their trains while others leisurely strolled, coffees in hand.

As he made his way back towards the station, he noticed a familiar figure leaning against a wall off to the side, deep in a phone conversation. As he approached, the voice became audible, and he realized it was Bibian laughing on the other end.

"Hold on, let me grab you a video message." She paused, standing on tiptoes to catch a glimpse of something just out of sight. Just then, she glanced up and noticed Ishiki trailing behind her, her eyes lighting up instantly. "Ishiki! I have to call you back; I just saw someone amazing!" she exclaimed, just as she disconnected the call.

"Someone amazing?" he questioned playfully, raising an eyebrow. "Who could that be?"

Before she could answer, out walked a tall figure from the crowd—a woman with spirited eyes and a cheerful demeanor, walking towards them. As she drew closer, Ishiki's heart skipped a beat. It was Yuki, and she looked radiant, bundled in a pastel coat adorned with reindeer details, her hair flowing freely down her shoulders.

"Yuki!" he called out, excitement bubbling within him as he jogged over to embrace his friend. "I didn't expect to see you here!"

"I planned a little holiday shopping!" she grinned, her face radiant with joy. "But I had the day off and couldn't resist getting into the holiday spirit. Plus, the bakery was calling my name!"

Bibian joined in on the hug, her petite frame nearly swallowed by the two taller friends. "What a coincidence! We've just picked up some delightful cakes for our Christmas gathering!"

Yuki's eyes sparkled at the mention of their plans. "What a surprise! I can't wait to see what you got! Are we going to try everything? We should have a mini feast right here and now!"

Ishiki chuckled, the warmth of their companionship settling over him like a cozy blanket in the midst of winter. "The bakery's offerings will have to wait; we still have time to prepare for the gathering. But I'm sure we can officially taste them together when everyone arrives."

"What are you two planning?" Yuki asked with a conspiratorial glance between them.

"We're also preparing to add some Taiwanese sweets to the mix," Bibian replied, practically bouncing in place. "I was just talking to my cousin earlier, and she said she'd share her family's secret recipe for egg tarts. It will be perfect for blending our cultures!"

"That sounds incredible!" Yuki enthusiastically exclaimed. "I love the idea of blending our culinary experiences. It'll bring so many flavors to our celebration!"

Ishiki chuckled at the sight of Bibian and Yuki, their animated conversation making plans for the gathering all the more exciting. "Let's incorporate some karaoke time into our celebration as well. After all, no Christmas is complete without a bit of singing."

"Perfect, I was hoping you would say that!" Bibian squeezed his arm in excitement. "And Akira will bring his guitar, right?"

Just then, the atmosphere shifted as they turned to exit the station. Out from the bustling crowd emerged Akira, holding a coffee cup and a couple of shopping bags. "I was hoping to run into you all!" he called out, effortlessly striding over to the group with his characteristic calmness.

"Akira! What have you found?" Yuki asked, curious about the items peeking from his bags.

"Oh, just some last-minute gifts," he chuckled, glancing at the conversation swirling around him. "And... a little something for the karaoke night—some new music!"

"Great! It's perfect!" Bibian exclaimed, her energy swiftly surrounding them. "We should incorporate our traditions into our karaoke too. It could be a fun way to end the night!"

"Exactly," Ishiki agreed, glancing at everyone gathered before him. "This gathering will be a celebration of flavors alongside great music, where we all share a piece of our home."

With each detail excitedly shared, the friends' anticipation grew, building upon every word exchanged. Ishiki couldn't help but feel that the reunion was merely the start of something magical, an unanticipated piece of a winter tapestry woven together by their shared experiences and their eagerness to learn from one another.

"Should we start gathering supplies for our cook-off?" Yuki proposed thoughtfully, her eyes dancing with enthusiasm. "We can write down a list and separate the tasks!"

"Absolutely! I can head to the supermarket for our ingredients," Ishiki offered, glancing at the cakes nestled under his arm. "It's a good excuse to try out new flavors."

"Perfect! I'll come along," Akira suggested, his face lighting up. "I've got a few recipes that could use some ingredients as well."

"I'll organize some decorations to keep our spirits high!" Bibian added with a bright grin. "Maybe we can hang some lights around Ishiki's place and make it festive."

As they continued down the bustling street, Ishiki felt a rush of gratitude swell within him. This unexpected reunion among friends had birthed new energy, reminiscent of the warmth and togetherness he admired in their cultures. Each of them brought something unique to the table—whether it was food, music, or simply laughter—that made the mundane feel extraordinary.

The camaraderie continued to grow as they strolled through the vibrant Nakamozu station, the sounds of laughter blending with the chatter of passersby. Along the way, they paused at stalls lined with handcrafted goods and trinkets, stopping occasionally to admire the seasonal decorations that adorned every corner.

As they reached the supermarket, the reality of their plans became tangible. They split up into teams as they traversed the aisles, gathering ingredients that would remind each of them of home. Bibian darted towards the sweets aisle, her eyes gleaming with joy as she picked up some ingredients to make traditional Taiwanese Christmas pastries, while Ishiki and Akira focused on the fresh produce and proteins needed for their dishes.

"I can't wait for everyone to experience tonight's flavors. I've been thinking of incorporating traditional Japanese seasonings into Bibian's egg tarts," Ishiki remarked as they placed their items in the cart.

"Perfect! That'll certainly fuse our customs," Akira added with a smile, his calm demeanor blending beautifully with the excitement in the air.

As they proceeded to the checkout, a sense of fulfillment settled in the group. They shared more ideas, teasing suggestions, and friendly banter, ensuring their gathering would encompass the very essence of their friendship—a fusion celebrating each other's traditions.

Once they'd completed their shopping, returning home filled with bags of ingredients and recipes, the laughter continued as they divided tasks. Bibian organized her plans for decoration and baked goods, while Yuki took over the culinary side, directing everyone on meal prep.

That evening, as they worked collaboratively in Ishiki's cozy apartment, the soft glow of twinkling lights adorning the walls and the fragrant aroma of simmering dishes filled the air. Akira strummed his guitar as they sang along to traditional carols, infusing their gathering with warmth and memories that wrapped around them like a comforting embrace.

With every dish they created and every song they sang, the unexpected reunion transformed into a cherished memory—a blending of cultures, friendships, and dreams. Ishiki smiled at the sight, feeling proud of how far they had come and how beautifully they had woven their lives together, each thread enriching the fabric of their shared story.

Later that evening, as they took their seats around the table filled with a fusion feast, Ishiki made a heartfelt toast, surrounded by his friends and the warmth of their cultures. "To new friendships, beautiful traditions, and the joy of coming together— may we always celebrate our stories, no matter where they lead us."

With laughter spilling over each beautifully crafted dish, the true essence of Christmas enveloped them as friends gathered closer, a celebration of life illuminated by shared experiences and collective dreams.

CHAPTER 4: BIBIAN'S FIRST IMPRESSIONS

The glow of the morning sun streamed through Ishiki's apartment windows, casting a warm, inviting light across the modest living room where the echoes of the previous evening's karaoke still hung thick in the air. Ishiki stood by the kitchen counter, pouring steaming hot tea into two ceramic cups, savoring the blend of jasmine and green that spoke of comfort and familiarity. He could hear the faint sound of Bibian's laughter through the thin walls, mixing with the aroma of breakfast frying on the stovetop.

"Good morning, sleepyhead!" he called out, his warm smile wide as Bibian emerged from her room, hair tumbling past her shoulders like a waterfall. She stretched, the energy of the morning brightening her petite frame with a burst of enthusiasm.

"Mmmm, morning! It feels like Christmas morning!" she exclaimed, her voice bubbling with cheer. "What smells so good?"

"Just some eggs and toast. Simple breakfast for a busy day of preparation," he replied, motioning for her to join him at the kitchen table that was cluttered with an assortment of ingredients they had prepared the night before for their Christmas gathering later that evening.

"Busy day indeed!" Bibian chirped as she grabbed a slice of toast, layering it with fresh avocado and a sprinkle of salt. "I can't wait to share your culture's Christmas traditions! I feel like I'm in a dream—Christmas in Japan with my favorite people."

Once they settled in for breakfast, the conversation flowed easily. Ishiki shared anecdotes from his childhood—how Christmas in Japan was often understated compared to the grand celebrations she described from Taiwan, focusing more on food than elaborate decorations. In Japan, the beautiful fried chicken became a staple, with families often gathering for a festive meal. Meanwhile, Bibian regaled Ishiki with stories about her aunt's extravagant Christmas parties, rich with Taiwanese culinary traditions, the warm glow of lanterns, and laughter echoing through the night.

"So, do people actually receive gifts here?" she asked, her eyes wide with curiosity.

"Not typically," Ishiki chuckled. "It's more about sharing food and experiences with those close to your heart. The New Year is when gifts are exchanged."

"I love that idea. It's all about celebrating together rather than the commercialism that can overshadow the holiday," Bibian said thoughtfully, her expression reflecting her eagerness to embrace this new experience.

After breakfast, they began their preparations, breaking out ingredients piled high across the island. Bibian insisted on making her famous Taiwanese egg tarts, her energy infectious. "They'll be a great addition!" she declared, dashing around the kitchen, her ponytail bouncing with every step.

"Sure, but do you need help?" Ishiki inquired, peering over at her.

"With egg tarts? Absolutely not!" she replied playfully, showcasing her confidence as she handed him a whisk. "But I could use a taste tester once they come out of the oven!"

Ishiki laughed, his heart swelling with admiration as she bustled about with an efficiency that was genuinely delightful. He reveled in their shared laughter, the vibrant colors of her cheerful clothing brightening the ambiance of his home and creating a sense of warmth often lacking in the cold Japanese winters.

As Bibian whisked the pastry, Ishiki couldn't help but admire the cultural blend taking shape between them. She hummed idly, mixing ingredients with a precision that belied her playful demeanor. Her spirit of innovation was infectious, and he found himself drawn into her narratives of Taiwanese customs intermingling seamlessly with Japanese traditions as they worked together in his cozy kitchen.

"You have to share your family's special recipes with me, too!" Ishiki urged, excited by the prospect of learning more about her culinary heritage. "This isn't just about sharing food today; it's about sharing stories that come with it."

"Oh, you bet!" Bibian grinned, looking up from her mixing bowl, a splash of egg yolk adorning her cheek. "I'd love to! The egg tarts have this history that goes back generations. My grandmother used to make them every Christmas, and they always brought the family together, kind of like your fried chicken!"

As the delicate pastry shells baked in the oven, the kitchen filled with delightful fragrances of butter and sweet cream. It sparked a conversation about their families, leading to heartwarming and sometimes bittersweet stories that further knit them together.

"Tell me more about your grandmother," Ishiki prompted as he carefully adjusted the temperature of the oven. "Was she the one who inspired your love of cooking?"

"Definitely!" Bibian replied, her voice brightening at the memory. "She loved cooking for everyone and telling stories while she helped us with the preparations. Every holiday was filled with laughter. The kitchen was her domain, and it was always a hive of activity. We used to argue over who would help, but in the end, it was really about being together."

"That sounds beautiful," Ishiki said softly, reflecting on the memories of his own family gatherings. "My mom used to make a spectacular matcha cake every year. It was that specific flavor that lives on in my heart."

"I must try your mother's cake! It's a tradition worth celebrating," Bibian exclaimed, her eyes twinkling. The warmth of their shared connection blossomed with every conversation, every slice of shared history.

As the timer on the oven pinged to life, Bibian rushed over with enthusiasm. She carefully pulled the golden-brown egg tarts from the oven. "Are you ready for this?"

"Absolutely! This moment is worthy of celebration in itself!" Ishiki replied, his heart swelling with anticipation.

The tarts glistened under the soft kitchen lights, steam swirling around them as they sat in their golden crusts. As Bibian carefully plated them, the initial excitement turned to wonder; the first taste held promise and nostalgia, with notes of sweet custard enveloped in a buttery embrace.

With the first bite, a chorus of flavors danced over Ishiki's palate; it was both rich and delicate. "Wow. These are incredible!" he exclaimed, a genuine smile stretching across his face. "I can see why the holidays demand these in your family!"

"Success!" Bibian celebrated, raising her pastry in joyous triumph. "Now we need to prepare your fried chicken for everyone else, so let's get to work!"

As they transitioned back to culinary collaboration, the apartment filled with laughter and delightful banter as they prepared the rest of the dishes.

Eventually, as the afternoon sun began to dip on the horizon, casting long shadows across the living room lined with cultural artifacts, the friends began to arrive. Yuki was the first, her bright pastel sweater shimmering even in the sunset glow.

"Is that the smell of egg tarts I sense?" she asked, bursting through the door with a dazzling smile, her warmth lighting the room. "I knew I smelled something incredible on my way up! Bibian's egg tarts smell divine."

"Bibian made them!" Ishiki exclaimed, motioning to Bibian who stood with her hands on her hips, beaming with pride.

"Really? You must teach me your secrets," Yuki replied, her enthusiasm mirroring Bibian's.

"Definitely! They're simple, really. Just a little patience and lots of love," Bibian replied, her animated fervor drawing everyone closer. "Come, try one!"

As Yuki helped herself to a tart, Akira arrived shortly after, his tall frame slipping into the space with a gentle smile. "I came as soon as I could. What did I miss?"

"Bibian's culinary mastery," Ishiki announced, gesturing toward the spread upon the table, where trays of fried chicken had also come together alongside the egg tarts. The room resonated with laughter and celebratory cheers as they engaged in warm hugs, excited to reconnect.

With everyone gathered around the table, they took turns sampling the array of delicious bites. Conversations flowed effortlessly, stories bubbling over with joy, misunderstandings into laughter, and reflections leading into shared cultural insights.

As Bibian watched the unfolding jubilation, her heart brimmed with gratitude. She felt the warmth of togetherness and acceptance, thriving amidst the fusion of their diverse heritages. The sparkling lights around the apartment created an aura of festivity, accentuating the harmonious blend of Christmas and Taiwanese customs that created a sense of belonging.

It dawned on her that Christmas in a foreign land could feel strangely familiar when surrounded by friends who had opened their hearts to her. In that moment, she reflected on the beautiful tapestry they had started to weave together via culinary exchanges, each thread representing their unique stories.

"Tonight is about more than just bringing our individual tastes together," Ishiki raised his glass, the sun dipping lower against the horizon, casting strands of light across the room. "It symbolizes the connections we are building through our friendship, culture, and food."

"Cheers to that!" The friends chimed in, raising their glasses high.

As dusk settled into twilight, the atmosphere filled with collective warmth from the hearth of their camaraderie, they celebrated the melding of traditions, the laughter echoing through Ishiki's apartment and into the future—a tapestry of memories and stories waiting to be exchanged, crafted within the bonds they were forging.

CHAPTER 5: FRIED CHICKEN AND FESTIVAL LIGHTS

The excitement in Ishiki's cozy apartment was palpable as Bibian entered the space, her small backpack slung over one shoulder, adorned with bright pins from her travels. The air was filled with a blend of savory and sweet as the warm scents of fried chicken wafted through the open kitchen. Yuki, who had arrived earlier, was arranging a festive display, her pastel accessories adding a cheerful vibrancy to the atmosphere.

"Yuki! You have outdone yourself with the decorations!" Bibian exclaimed, her expressive eyes widening at the sight of strings of colorful lights and handmade paper ornaments adorning the walls, casting a soft glow that echoed the warmth of the season.

Yuki grinned as she fastened the final touches to a paper crane between two large holiday banners. "I wanted to create a festive atmosphere for our gathering! It's all about celebrating togetherness and sharing traditions, right?"

"Absolutely!" Bibian chirped, swinging her backpack off and setting it down with a soft thud. "Have you already prepped the special dishes you mentioned?"

"Almost! I've got the sweet potato salad simmering, and I'll whip up some ginger-flavored rice shortly," Yuki replied, excitement bubbling in her tone. "But I'll need some help too. There's simply so much to do before everyone arrives!"

Ishiki, who had been busy prepping the chicken, looked over his shoulder with a grin. "How about I help you with the rice while Bibian takes care of your egg tarts? A true collaboration."

"Perfect! I'll show you the recipe for my special sticky ginger rice," Yuki said, her enthusiasm infectious.

"Sounds delicious!" Bibian added, her ponytail flicking back as she grabbed the ingredients from her backpack. "And I'm so ready to make those egg tarts shine!"

While they settled into their kitchen roles, the atmosphere came alive with laughter and playful banter. Ishiki and Yuki worked together, carefully measuring and mixing the ingredients for the rice, while Bibian focused intently on her egg tarts, her small frame encompassed by the warm glow of the kitchen lights.

"Have you ever made egg tarts before?" Bibian peeked over her shoulder as she rolled out the delicate pastry dough.

"No, this is my first time. I usually cook savory dishes," Ishiki replied, concentrating on keeping the rice from sticking to the pot. "But I'm excited to learn from you! The way you describe the flavors makes me want to taste every bite."

Bibian chuckled as she dashed back to her mixing bowl, meticulously preparing the filling. "It's all about balance—sweetness from the eggs, the flaky texture of the crust, and a hint of vanilla that dances on your tongue. You'll love it!"

As they divided their tasks, the sound of sizzling oil accompanied their conversations, the savory aroma of fried chicken enveloping the room as it fried to golden perfection. It was a dish Ishiki had prepared countless times over the years, and he loved how it became a staple during Christmas, reminiscent of the warmth and laughter shared among family and friends.

"I can't believe how much I've learned from everyone!" Bibian shared as she prepared to place her tarts into the oven. "It's incredible how our cultures mesh through food."

"It really is," Yuki added thoughtfully, stirring the pot of rice. "In Japan, we have a tradition of eating fried chicken for Christmas—something that began as an adaptation of Western customs, evolving into a festive feast we all cherish."

"Fried chicken with rice sounds like a perfect combo!" Bibian said, her voice brimming with excitement. "I love how these unconventional pairings bring everyone together and create an experience that's distinctly ours."

As they chatted, the kitchen transformed into a tapestry of cultural exchanges. Laughter weaved through the air, each story shared wound tighter into the fabric of their friendship, merging their traditions into one beautiful gathering.

With the aromas lingering in the air, they moved to arrange the table, Yuki adding decorative pieces while Ishiki prepared to set the dishes. Bibian popped her egg tarts out of the oven, the sweet scent wafting over to the table, making the perfect accompaniment to Ishiki's succulent fried chicken.

"Look at that golden perfection!" Ishiki declared, mesmerized as he plated the chicken. "We're about to have ourselves a feast!"

As they finished their preparations, Akira arrived, his tall frame filling the entrance of Ishiki's apartment. "Sorry I'm late! I got caught up at work," he said, but his voice was upbeat.

"You're just in time!" Yuki exclaimed, gesturing towards the table. "We were just about to enjoy this amazing feast we've created together."

"I had a feeling the best company would be here," he replied with a smile, stepping in fully and taking a moment to appreciate the festive ambiance.

The friends gathered around the table, their excitement building as the dishes were unveiled. Ishiki's fried chicken glistening temptingly beside Bibian's light egg tarts and Yuki's portion of ginger rice, all sitting atop a colorful spread of side dishes.

"I can't wait to dig in!" Akira said with an appreciative grin, "This looks amazing! Can we toast before we start?"

They all nodded enthusiastically. Ishiki retrieved some glasses and poured a special sparkling drink Yuki had prepared, adding to the celebratory tone of their gathering.

"To new friendships, cherished traditions, and the joy of coming together—may we share many more meals like this!" Ishiki declared, lifting his glass high.

The others followed suit, clinking their glasses together. "Cheers!" they chorused.

As they began digging into the dishes, the conversation flowed again—a mix of playful jabs about who had the best recipe and joyful stories of past Christmases.

"I really love the crispy outside of your fried chicken!" Bibian grinned as she savored her first bite. "It has such great seasoning! What do you add?"

"Just a few spices," Ishiki smiled, enjoying her delight. "The secret ingredient is always love!"

Yuki raised an eyebrow playfully. "All food tastes better with love! Right, Bibian?"

"Right! I'm glad I brought the egg tarts—for sweetness and warmth!"

They all burst into laughter, their faces glowing in the lights that adorned the room. The food acted as a backdrop to the unfolding stories, each dish reflecting the companionship and shared energy that surrounded them.

With each plate emptied and filled again, the evening unfolded—a festival of flavors, laughter, and shared memories. They reminisced about holiday traditions, amusing anecdotes, and their favorite foods across various cultures.

Finally, as they settled back in their seats, full and satisfied, the energy shifted slightly to a more reflective tone. "You know," Akira said pensively, "I really appreciate these moments with all of you. Christmas is more than just a holiday; it's about the connections we make."

"Exactly," Bibian chimed in, her voice warm. "I've felt how these culinary experiences have drawn us closer. They're more than just a meal; they transform into beautiful memories we'll carry together."

Yuki nodded, taking in the sentiments as she admired the sparkling lights. "And it's so important to pass on these traditions to others, to keep sharing our stories and our cultures."

"Let's not forget about karaoke!" Ishiki said with a playful grin, breaking the moment of reflection. "We must continue the celebrations with some festive singing!"

Bibian lit up, her energetic spirit back. "I've been eagerly waiting for this! Let's pull out the songbooks and get ready for an amazing karaoke party!"

With a sense of jubilance, they cleared the table and prepared the karaoke machine, the atmosphere shifting from satisfied calmness to buoyant energy again.

As the music filled the room and their voices harmonized with the cheerful melodies, the spirit of Christmas enveloped them all. From Bibian's spirited renditions of Taiwanese pop songs to Ishiki's soulful takes on traditional Japanese ballads, the night transformed into a symphony of joyful harmony.

In each song, layers of culture unfurled and intertwined, a testament to the friendships forged in love and laughter—they came together to celebrate more than just Christmas; they celebrated the beauty of unity amidst diversity.

As they sang their hearts out, laughter echoed through the walls, resounding far beyond the confines of Ishiki's apartment. It was a night where their separate traditions became one enchanting evening, lighting up the surroundings like the shimmering festival lights adorning the room.

Together, they created their narrative, partaking in the magical essence of their individual journeys and celebrating the wonderful blend they had cultivated through food, songs, and laughter—a reminder that true connection transcends borders, binding them together in the tapestry of cherished memories they would carry into the future.

CHAPTER 6: SWEET MOMENTS IN NAKAMOZU

The morning sun spilled into Ishiki's apartment, bathing the cozy living space in a warm, golden glow. The quiet hum of the world outside felt almost distant as Bibian busily arranged the final touches for their Christmas gathering later that day. She was a whirlwind of energy, her petite frame darting around, carrying decorations and placing them around the room with careful thought.

"Ishiki! Have you seen those tiny ornaments I brought?" Bibian called out, her ponytail bobbing as she stretched up to hang a string of lights from the edge of the shelf. "They'll look amazing right here next to the photos!"

"Check the dining table! I think you left them there while we were unpacking earlier," Ishiki replied, his voice blending amusement with fondness as he watched her.

As she rummaged through the remnants of the festive supplies scattered over the table, Ishiki couldn't help but smile. The vibrant colors and textures of Bibian's offerings created a delightful contrast to the cultural artifacts that filled his home— each photograph and decorative piece telling a story of shared experiences and cherished memories.

"Found it!" Bibian's voice rang out, holding up a small box of glimmering ornaments that reflected the sunlight, scattering little sparks of light over the walls. As she carefully unwrapped them, her eyes sparkled with enthusiasm. "These are from my last trip to Taiwan! They remind me of home, especially during the holidays. I thought they would add a special touch to your place."

"I love them!" Ishiki said, keen to see how she would integrate her lively spirit into his home. He glanced around, appreciating how their individual styles were merging into one beautiful tapestry celebrating their cultures.

Bibian began placing the ornaments with meticulous attention, turning every corner into a visual delight. "I can't wait for Yuki and Akira to arrive! I hope they love the decorations. And let's not forget the cakes!"

Their conversation drifted effortlessly as they worked together, discussions punctuated with laughter and encouragement. The air was vibrant with the scent of freshly brewed coffee and sweet pastries, which blended beautifully with the crisp winter air wafting in from the slightly open window.

"Do you think we should save a slice of that matcha cake for later? It might serve us well as a sweet surprise after we finish cooking!" Bibian suggested, her eyes gleaming with mischief.

Ishiki chuckled as he lifted the decorated cake off the table and carefully placed it on a higher shelf, separating it from the bustling activities of the kitchen. "We'll need it for our festive moment—the grand reveal with all the friends gathered. This matcha cake will be our shining star!"

"Agreed! And I'm sure they'll love the egg tarts too," she replied, her voice lilting with enthusiasm. "It's all about sharing those sweet moments together, right?"

As they chatted, the doorbell chimed, breaking through their rhythmic preparation. Ishiki's heart raced with excitement. The energy had been building for days, and the time for their gathering had finally arrived.

"I'll get it!" Bibian exclaimed, dashing for the door while Ishiki grabbed a couple of cups to prepare for the first guests.

As the door swung open, Yuki stood there, her beaming smile brightening the entryway, adorned in an outfit that perfectly matched the festive spirit of the occasion. "Merry Christmas, you two!" she exclaimed, stepping inside with an air of joy, her pastel sweater gleaming.

"Merry Christmas!" Ishiki and Bibian chorused, embracing her warmly.

"Wow, the apartment looks incredible! I love what you've done with the decorations, Bibian! They add such a vibrant touch to the space," Yuki said, marveling at the enchanting atmosphere.

"It's a team effort—come help me with the food while you admire it!" Bibian replied, already gesturing for Yuki to follow her into the kitchen.

As they moved to the kitchen area, the hum of chatter rose as the trio caught up, excitement thickening in the air. Bibian began to explain her plan for the festive spread. "We're preparing traditional fried chicken and the most delicious egg tarts for dessert. I'll guide you through my family recipe!"

"Sounds amazing! Can I help with the egg tarts?" Yuki asked, her eyes sparkling. "I've always wanted to learn how to make them!"

"Of course! We'll need all the hands we can get," Bibian chuckled, thankful for her friend's eagerness to jump in. "But first, let's make sure the preparations for the fried chicken go smoothly. Ishiki already prepped the chicken—thank you for that!"

"Anything to help my friends," he said modestly, smiling as he moved to grab the well-seasoned chicken pieces from the refrigerator and passed them over.

Just as the laughter and chatter filled the kitchen, Akira's tall figure appeared in the doorway, balancing a guitar case slung over his shoulder and a small box decorated with a festive bow in his hands. "Hey everyone! Sorry I'm late; I got held up at work. What's this about egg tarts?" he joked, a grin spreading across his face as he entered.

"Merry Christmas, Akira!" they all chimed in unison. Yuki rushed over, pulling him into a warm embrace while Bibian bounced with eagerness.

"Since you're here now, you're just in time to help with the egg tarts! Yuki is all in for learning how to make them, and it'll be hilarious if you join us!" Bibian beckoned, her infectious excitement making everyone grin.

"Learning to cook with the two of you is always something I'm game for!" Akira chuckled, his calm demeanor complementing their vibrant energy. He settled in beside Yuki and began to survey the ingredients laid out.

As the preparations kicked into high gear, the kitchen became a canvas of creativity. Bibian demonstrated how to make the pastry crust, her hands deftly mixing flour and butter with cheerful chatter. Yuki leaned in closely, watching the motions with rapt concentration while Akira strummed his guitar idly, adding whimsy to the atmosphere.

"Did you know this is my grandmother's famous egg tart recipe? It's a family secret passed down for generations!" Bibian explained, her lips breaking into a smile as she showed them how to roll and cut the pastry into perfect circles.

"I love that you're sharing this tradition! Every bite will carry a piece of your heritage with it," Yuki emphasized, appreciating the honor Bibian was bestowing by sharing something so meaningful.

As they continued, the laughter and energy radiated through the kitchen. Ishiki moved around the space, flipping chicken in a hot pan and grabbing drinks from the fridge while keeping a careful eye on the array of dishes coming together.

"Hey! Make sure not to skimp on the sugar in the custard," Bibian called over her shoulder, elbow-deep in flour and smiles.

"I promise, sweet doesn't skip my mind," he teased back, chuckling before concentrating on the chicken sizzling away.

After several rounds of cheerful banter and delicious chaos in the kitchen, the delicious aroma of fried chicken filled every corner of the apartment. The blend of sweet and savory teased their senses, heightening the anticipation for the gathering ahead.

"Can you smell that? It's incredible!" Akira exclaimed, his eyes wide in appreciation. He put his guitar down for a moment to reposition a bowl filled with the tart mixture. "It might be too early to eat, but I must admit I'm feeling hungry already."

As the egg tarts began to bake in the oven, rich scents began filling the air, mingling with the lingering smells of the fried chicken. Ishiki gathered the decorative components, beginning to set the table and creating a cozy space for their friends to gather.

"Okay, we need to assemble everything with love and care. Doesn't it feel like Christmas is truly here now?" he said, his heart swelling with warmth at the sight of his friends working diligently and happily side by side.

Bibian's laughter rang through the air as she reached for the ornaments they had hung earlier. "Absolutely! All this effort makes it feel like we're carrying each other's traditions forward, cherishing them along the way."

As they continued arranging the table, every line and detail echoed their growing bond. The sun had dipped lower in the sky, casting a warm glow through the window, creating a sense of intimacy that filled the space.

Finally, they settled at the table, fixing the last details of their spread. The festive decorations surrounded the food—a beautiful array of fried chicken and golden egg tarts, a sweet matcha cake ready for dessert, and an array of colorful plates filling the table.

"I think we're ready for the grand reveal," Bibian said, her eyes glowing with excitement.

Ishiki nodded, looking at each of his friends who had put their hearts into these dishes. "Let's welcome our other friends and share this moment together!"

With a flourish, he opened the door as more friends entered the cozy atmosphere of his apartment, laughter and cheer bursting in like a welcome breath of fresh air. More welcoming hugs were exchanged, and as everyone took their seats, a sense of belonging settled over the room.

"To our friendship and celebrating the unique blend of our cultures," Ishiki proclaimed, raising his glass. "May we cherish each sweet moment together, weaving our stories into a beautiful tapestry!"

With glasses raised and the room echoing their laughter and joy, it dawned on each of them that it was more than just the food—it was the connections they were forging, the traditions they were embracing, and the memories they were creating.

As they laughed and shared stories over delicious bites, every item on the table echoed their journey together. Christmas, filled with warmth and the sweet flavors of their fusions, became more than a celebration; it became a celebration of life—a dedication to friendship that was destined to intertwine them all.

Time faded away in that cozy apartment, each moment stretching into countless sweet memories, connecting every rhythm of their hearts. One bite, one song, and one shared experience at a time, they sparked joy, creating the magic of the season within their laughter and love.

CHAPTER 7: A CHRISTMAS CAKE CONUNDRUM

The following day dawned with a crisp chill in the air, the sun painting a delicate frost over the streets of Nakamozu. As the bustling sounds of people hurrying to work filled the train station nearby, Ishiki Nakamura awoke in his cozy apartment, the tantalizing scent of freshly brewed coffee wafting through the air. He squinted against the light filtering through his living room window, scattered across the eclectic tapestry of cultural artifacts that adorned his home.

Yesterday had been a blend of laughter, food, and shared traditions, culminating in a beautiful celebration that had woven their diverse cultural threads into a colorful fabric of memory. Ishiki felt invigorated, ready to embrace the day and celebrate once more with his friends, particularly with Christmas just a week away. There was a plan to finalize today: selecting the perfect Christmas cake to serve at their upcoming gathering.

"Bibian, are you ready?" he called out with a hint of excitement in his voice.

From the small kitchenette, Bibian's cheerful response echoed back, filled with the same enthusiasm. "Just about! I'm looking forward to our cake adventure today!" Her voice was buoyant, radiating her signature energy, and Ishiki couldn't help but smile as he pulled on his favorite hoodie over his jeans.

After a quick breakfast and a brew of steaming coffee for himself, Ishiki cleared the table and put on his shoes, ready to head out. Today was important; not only would they be selecting the cake for their Christmas celebration, but they also planned to document their culinary journey to share with others. Bibian had suggested posting their experiences on social media, and Ishiki thought that sounded like a splendid idea. He had grown fond of capturing moments and sharing them with their friends and followers, especially moments that embodied the unity of cultures they were celebrating.

When they reached the local Japanese bakery—a quaint little place adorned with festive lights and decorations—Bibian's eyes lit up at the sight of the colorful assortment of cakes displayed in the storefront window. "Look at all of these! They're so beautiful!" she exclaimed, her petite figure bouncing on her heels.

Ishiki chuckled, enjoying watching her unfettered enthusiasm. "This is one of my favorite bakeries. They make the best Christmas cakes, but I'm curious to see what you think of them."

Stepping into the bakery, they were immediately enveloped by the sweet aroma of freshly baked goods mixed with holiday spices. The air was alive with the sounds of cheerful chatter as customers perused through the display, and the warm ambiance felt like a welcoming embrace.

"Would you like to try a sample, my dear?" an elderly lady behind the counter asked, her smile wide and wrinkled with years of joy. She had seen countless customers come through this bakery, each with a story to share and memories to create.

"Yes, please!" Bibian replied eagerly, leaning in closer to the counter where an array of beautifully decorated cakes beckoned. There was the classic strawberry shortcake, adorned with seasonal fruits and fluffy whipped cream, as well as rich chocolate ganache cakes that glistened invitingly.

"Each of these cakes has something special to offer," Ishiki explained, pointing to the matcha cake that brought a fond smile to his face. "This one is traditional for Christmas in Japan, with layers rich in flavor and subtle sweetness. It's always a crowd favorite."

As they deliberated, Bibian wavered between the festive flavors. "I love the fusion of tastes! But I'm also excited to try something distinctly Japanese," she mused. "What if we combine our cultures and have a cake that symbolizes our experiences?"

Ishiki perked up at her intriguing idea. "I love that! A blend of Taiwanese and Japanese flavors could be remarkable. But can they do it here?"

"Let's ask!" Bibian replied, her excitement bubbling over as she approached the counter.

"Excuse me," she began, her warm smile radiating her eagerness. "This might sound a bit unusual, but is there any way we could create a cake that merges elements from both Taiwanese and Japanese traditions?"

The baker, her kind eyes sparkling with a hint of intrigue, nodded thoughtfully. "Absolutely! We love custom orders! What do you have in mind?"

Feeling invigorated by the friendly rapport, Ishiki joined in, "Maybe a matcha-infused layer combined with a creamy egg tart center? We could top it with fresh fruits—like strawberries and mangoes?"

"That sounds delightful!" the baker exclaimed, her face lighting up with enthusiasm. "I can see this cake bridging both cultures beautifully. How about we add a layer of fluffy whipped cream on top for that festive finish?"

Bibian clapped her hands with glee. "Yes! I can already envision it! This is going to be the highlight of our celebration!"

After discussing the details and placing their order, they strolled leisurely through the bakery, sampling sweet pastries and enjoying their favorite chocolate-covered dorayaki. They made sure to grab a couple of egg tarts, still warm from the oven, that Bibian insisted on showcasing in her upcoming posts.

"Food brings people together, doesn't it?" she said, savoring every bite. "I love how we can blend flavors and create something entirely new together."

"I agree," Ishiki replied, a smile lighting up his face. "And the beauty of it lies in the stories we share while exploring these tastes. Like how we became friends over shared meals and traditions."

With their newfound culinary adventure in mind, they meandered back toward Ishiki's apartment, relishing every moment filled with light-hearted banter. As they entered, Bibian whipped out her phone excitedly, ready to capture the magic they had just experienced.

"Let's document the process as we prepare for the gathering! First, the cake reveal!" she declared, her enthusiasm infectious.

They prepared a workspace in the living room, placing the box containing the half-finished cake in the center of the table, surrounded by ingredients for the decoration and additional festive treats Bibian had brought with her.

"Okay! What's next on our agenda?" Ishiki asked, chuckling at her zesty energy. "Are we assembling it right away?"

"Let's get creative!" she chirped, grabbing a piping bag designed for decorating, ready to frost the cake once it cooled. "But first, remember we need to prepare the matcha cream filling. I'll handle that while you handle the whipped cream."

With Bibian leading the way, they grabbed their ingredients and began the whirlwind of activity that would fill Ishiki's apartment with laughter and the sweet scent of culinary creation. Bibian whisked the cream and matcha, talking animatedly about her plans for their further social media posts, which would include snippets of their Christmas journey together.

"People love seeing how food allows us to connect and share stories," she said, pouring the matcha mixture into a bowl. "We can show them the joy of crossing cultures through food."

"Absolutely! Showcase the essence of our gathering and how each layer of the cake represents our unique traditions," Ishiki replied, his heart resonating with enthusiasm at the thought.

The two friends worked side by side, Ishiki whipping the cream until soft peaks formed, while Bibian carefully folded the vibrant green matcha mixture into the fluffy texture. With little bursts of laughter and playful comments, their bond grew stronger with each passing moment.

"Here comes the fun part!" Bibian waved the spatula dramatically as she finished preparing the matcha cream. "Let's assemble this masterpiece!"

Together, they placed the light and fluffy layers on the table, arranging them with precision, taking care to evenly distribute their creations. As Bibian layered the matcha cream within the cake, Ishiki felt a sense of joy radiating in the atmosphere around them.

"Just look at these colors! It's a true representation of our personalities coming together," Bibian declared, a swirl of matcha cream coating the star of the show beautifully.

"Exactly! Now for the final flourish—let's top it with those fresh fruits!" Ishiki said. They meticulously arranged slices of strawberries and mango atop their creation, the colors dancing with vibrancy against the creamy green of the matcha.

"Who knew we could create such a stunning Christmas cake together!" Bibian exclaimed, stepping back to admire their handiwork.

"I have to admit," Ishiki chuckled, looking at the final product, "this cake is truly a representation of us. Bright, unique, and a bit adventurous!"

After the cake was carefully decorated and tucked away in the refrigerator to set, they felt a wave of satisfaction sweep over them. Bibian clicked pictures to add to her blog, capturing the vibrancy of their Christmas spirit.

"Look how great this looks! Everyone will be excited to see this unique cake! We need to show it off during our gathering over the weekend," she exclaimed as she reviewed the photos.

"Speaking of our gathering, what do you have in mind for our karaoke set?" Ishiki inquired, keen to build on their previous celebration.

Bibian thought for a moment as she scrolled through her phone. "Karaoke! We need a mix of traditional tunes and upbeat holiday songs. Maybe even a couple of popular Taiwanese ones?"

"Perfect! Sounds like we're set for an incredible night ahead. And now we have this amazing cake to showcase." Ishiki felt a warm glow inside from the energy radiating between them; it was moments like these that cultivated the spirit of community and friendship.

The two spent the remainder of the afternoon planning songs for the karaoke party and sharing laughs over their favorite holiday memories.

As dusk settled over Nakamozu, Ishiki felt fortunate. The cake they crafted together was not just a dessert—it was a testament to their growing friendship, encapsulating the essence of the cultures they were blending into something purely delightful. And just like the process of preparing that cake, he knew each new day would bring the chance to savor life and connect, stitch by colorful stitch, into their shared narrative— a patchwork that made their hearts grow warmer even amid the chill of winter.

With Christmas around the corner, excitement bubbled within Ishiki and Bibian, fueling the anticipation for the gathering and the sweet, heartfelt moments yet to come. On the backdrop of the impending festivities lay the promise that through every slice shared, they would continue weaving their inspiring tapestry of culture and friendship.

CHAPTER 8: TRADITIONS TRANSFORMED

As the festive lights surrounding Nakamozu Station twinkled against the backdrop of a deepening twilight, the air buzzed with anticipation. Ishiki Nakamura stood at the station entrance, adjusting the collar of his favorite hoodie. A soft wind tousled his short black hair, bringing with it the promise of a beautiful evening.

He had invited Bibian, Yuki, and Akira to join him for a special excursion—an exploration of how Christmas was celebrated in various parts of Japan and Taiwan. The blend of cultures ignited excitement within him, prompting him to delve deeper into the traditions they had all begun embracing.

"Hey, Ishiki!" Bibian's enthusiastic voice broke through his thoughts as she approached, her long black hair trailing behind her in a lively ponytail. She wore a bright, festive sweater that perfectly matched her vibrant spirit. "Are you ready for our cultural adventure?"

"Absolutely! The places we're visiting tonight are a small representation of Christmas traditions in Japan and Taiwan," Ishiki replied, grinning as he gestured towards the ticket machine. "Let's grab our tickets and get going! Akira and Yuki are already on their way!"

Bibian clapped her hands, her excitement palpable. "I can't wait to see how both cultures celebrate this holiday. I've been hearing so much about Japanese melty cheese cakes, but I want to experience the whole essence of Christmas over here!"

As they procured their tickets, the sound of laughter caught Ishiki's ear. He turned to see Yuki and Akira hustling toward them, smiles brightening their faces.

"Sorry we're late! Yuki had to make some last-minute adjustments with her festive outfit," Akira joked, nodding toward Yuki, who blushed as she turned her head shyly.

"Well, someone has to look cute while we explore!" Yuki retorted playfully, a pastel scarf wrapped snugly around her neck. "But I'm ready now! What's the first stop?"

"Right here at Nakamozu! We'll take a train to Shibuya. It's known for its bustling atmosphere during Christmas, and there's a spectacular illumination display," Ishiki said, as he pointed toward the station's sign.

"Perfect! Let's soak in the holiday spirit!" Bibian declared, her energy transporting them all to a place where curiosity intertwined seamlessly with joy.

As they boarded the train, the soft chatter of passengers filled the air, mingling with the sounds of their excitement. "Do you have any favorite festive memories from Taiwan, Bibian?" Yuki inquired, her expression interested.

"Definitely! Christmas in Taiwan is not a public holiday, but we celebrate it in our own way. Families gather to have dinner together and exchange gifts. The decorations are bright and colorful. We might not have snow, but the streets come alive, and everyone embraces the lively spirit!" Bibian shared, her eyes lighting up as she regaled them with tales of family dinners filled with laughter and love.

"That sounds delightful!" Ishiki remarked, his passion for cultures evident as he fully listened. "In Japan, Christmas has taken on a unique flavor too. Many people enjoy fried chicken, while Christmas cakes are a must. It's fascinating how the holiday transforms across different cultures."

Akira leaned in, his calm demeanor adding depth to their conversation. "The emphasis on food and community during holidays is a universal theme. It shows how we celebrate and cherish each other's presence, regardless of where we come from," he reflected thoughtfully.

Bibian nodded, her expressive eyes shimmering with enthusiasm. "Cooking together and sharing meals with friends and family are what make any celebration even better!"

The train sped through the city, the scenery shifting as they neared Shibuya, the excitement bubbling evermore. Stepping out, the group was greeted by a dazzling spectacle of twinkling lights. The famous Shibuya Crossing was alive with holiday cheer, as throngs of people mingled in a sea of illuminated surroundings.

"Look at all those lights!" Yuki said, her voice full of wonder as she raised her smartphone to capture the beauty before her. "It's breathtaking!"

Swaying with the crowd, they made their way toward the massive Christmas tree decorated with bright ornaments and twinkling fairy lights. Bibian beamed as she stood before it, marveling at the beauty. "This reminds me of home, but even more magical! The spirit of celebration is so strong here!"

"That's the beauty of merging cultures," Ishiki observed, watching as Bibian reveled in the moment. "Japanese Christmas lights have come to represent both joy and hope, much like how you describe celebrations in Taiwan."

They took turns capturing photos, laughter echoing through the crisp night as they snapped selfies with the bustling backdrop of the tree. "We need to make a memory with this!" Bibian declared, making sure they all huddled together before clicking the shutter.

As they continued through the streets of Shibuya, they stumbled upon a holiday market brimming with stalls offering seasonal delights—think steaming mugs of hot chocolate, sweet treats, and savory snacks. "How about a little food exploration?" Yuki suggested, her eyes dancing with excitement at the sight of a stall adorned with colorful lanterns.

"Let's start with sweet potato balls. I came across a post that said they're a local favorite during the holidays!" Bibian eagerly exclaimed, leading the way.

After indulging in sweet potato balls—crispy on the outside and fluffy within—the group wandered further into the market, their senses mesmerized by the array of scents and colors. A stall decorated with aromatic roasted chestnuts caught Akira's attention. "Let's grab some of these! They're a winter staple in Japan," he said, pointing at the vendor.

With snacks in hand, they roamed the market, shareable laughter flowing easily among them. Every food stall became a treasure hunt, revealing not only tastes but also shared stories that deepened their bond.

"So, who's up for caroling?" Bibian asked playfully, her eyes twinkling like the lights around them.

They chuckled, but before anyone could respond, Bibian began to hum a cheerful melody. "I mean, it wouldn't be Christmas without a little singing, right?"

Embarrassed but amused, Yuki joined in, her voice rising above the chatter as the others followed suit. "We should embrace the spirit! Maybe even add a Taiwanese Christmas song into the mix?"

As they sang together, an unexpected camaraderie blossomed out of their playful banter and silly dance moves. The joy radiating from the group attracted smiles from passersby, who couldn't resist joining in the merriment.

When their song came to an end, the warmth of their shared experience felt tangible, creating a deep sense of connection among the group. "Do you see how music transcends all barriers? Just like food, it brings us together!" Yuki reflected, looking around at their growing audience.

With spirits lifted, they continued their journey through the market, until they reached a cozy café showcasing a mix of Taiwanese and Japanese pastries. "Let's take a break! I'm dying to try those taiyaki filled with matcha and sweet red bean," Ishiki suggested, eyeing a nearby display.

They settled in at a small corner table, warms drinks steaming in front of them. "This is such a perfect moment. Blending traditions not only deepens our understanding of each other but also allows us to create new experiences," Akira mused, looking around at the cozy café filled with stories resonating behind every sweet treat.

"Right? We're not just sampling food; we're tasting memories," Bibian chimed in. "Each bite unfolds a tale, echoing the beauty of our connections."

As they savored their treats, Bibian pulled out her laptop. "Let's document this adventure—what we've learned today about each other's cultures!" She tapped away energetically as the others gathered around.

They shared their favorite moments of the night: Bibian reminiscing about her family celebrations, Yuki recalling her unique cake recipes, Ishiki discussing the innovations in traditional food, and Akira connecting the layers of culture that brought warmth to their home.

"I never appreciated how interconnected our traditions are until tonight," Ishiki said, reflecting on their discussions. "We have so much richness in our various practices, yet we find warmth in one another's hearts."

Bibian nodded. "And every story we share is a thread that weaves our experiences into a beautiful tapestry."

After hours of wandering and sharing stories, the group had discovered a piece of themselves in each other, forming a bond that transcended cultural divides. As they prepared to leave the café, Bibian stood up, her eyes filled with determination. "Let's promise to embrace our unique traditions and continually invent new ones together. We should create our own blend of holiday celebrations!"

"That sounds wonderful!" Yuki added, her face animated with excitement.

"I love that idea! We can plan for future gatherings, blending what we cherish from Japan and Taiwan," Akira agreed.

Ishiki's heart swelled with pride. "It's about transforming our experiences into something beautiful. Each holiday we spend together will carry a part of who we are, reflecting our shared journeys."

As night deepened around them, they made their way out of the café and back into the bustling streets of Shibuya, excitement buoying their steps. They laughed and sang as they returned to the illumination display, their hearts full of warmth and smiles illuminated by twinkling lights.

With each step through the vibrant streets, their friendships blossomed like the brilliant displays around them, each one echoing the unity they had nurtured through their diverse traditions.

"Guys, let's take one last photo together!" Bibian suggested, enthusiastic about capturing yet another cherished memory.

They huddled beneath the grand Christmas tree one last time, the lights dancing above them, their faces lit by joy. As the camera clicked, they froze in the moment, savoring the thrill of kinship that now intertwined them evermore.

This Christmas and celebration of traditions wasn't merely an act; it had transformed into a shared narrative of friendship—an intertwining of stories and cultures that would flow into the future.

Tonight, they had taken those invaluable lessons and woven them into their hearts. Each moment they cherished became a spark—an inspiration for future seasons to come, reminding them always of their journey together, crafting a cool cultural fusion of joy and love, one celebration at a time.

CHAPTER 9: TAIPEI TALES AND TEAS

The crisp winter morning greeted Ishiki with a gentle chill as he pulled back the curtains of his apartment, allowing the soft light to fill the cozy space. Today was particularly exciting; Bibian had suggested they delve deeper into her Taiwanese traditions, focusing specifically on holiday teas and tales from her hometown. With Christmas a mere week away, Ishiki felt energized by the prospect of their cultural exploration.

As he brewed a cup of green tea for himself, the aroma wafted through the room, mingling with the remnants of the previous night's gathering. The laughter and camaraderie they had shared lingered in the air like warmth, fueling his anticipation for the day ahead. Just as he was preparing to sit down with his drink, he heard a lively knock at the door.

"Coming!" he called, setting his teacup down and moving towards the entrance. When he opened the door, he was greeted by Bibian's bright smile, her long hair cascading down her shoulders, bouncing as she shifted energetically on her feet.

"Good morning, Ishiki! I brought some special tea leaves for our adventure today!" she exclaimed, holding up a small, intricately decorated pouch adorned with floral patterns.

"Good morning, Bibian! What a delightful way to start the day!" Ishiki replied, a smile forming on his lips as he ushered her inside. "What kind of tea did you bring?"

"This is high mountain oolong tea from my hometown in Taiwan! It's really famous because of its unique flavor and aroma," she declared proudly, her eyes sparkling with enthusiasm. "I thought we could brew it and enjoy it while chatting about our Christmas tales!"

"Sounds perfect! Let's brew some now," Ishiki suggested, leading Bibian into the kitchen, where the morning light highlighted a small assortment of teapots—a collection he had started due to his fascination with different tea cultures.

As they prepared the tea together, Bibian explained the intricacies of the oolong variety. "Oolong is partially oxidized, so it has this wonderful balance between black and green teas. When brewed properly, it offers a rich, floral aroma and a sweet aftertaste." She watched as Ishiki measured the leaves with skillful hands. "You're going to love it!"

Once the water was ready, they steeped the leaves, and soon the kitchen filled with the intoxicating scent of the tea. "I can already smell the sweetness," Ishiki remarked, leaning closer to the pot.

"I feel the same way whenever I visit home during the holidays," Bibian mused, the warmth in her voice revealing her nostalgia. "In Taiwan, Christmas isn't a public holiday, but my family and I still make it special with our own traditions."

"What do you typically do?" Ishiki asked, his curiosity piqued.

Bibian's face brightened as she shared, "Well, my family loves to gather for a big dinner. We have hot pot, which is our version of comfort food. Everyone contributes ingredients that we cook together in a bubbling pot right at the table. It's a time for chatting, sharing stories, and enjoying each other's company. After that, we usually exchange small gifts."

"That sounds delightful! It really mirrors the spirit of Christmas," Ishiki replied, sipping on the freshly brewed tea. The flavor lingered beautifully on his palate, and he savored it as he listened intently. "Do you have a favorite gift that you've received?"

Bibian laughed lightly, causing the warmth from her personality to resonate throughout the kitchen. "Oh, yes! Last year, my mother surprised me with a beautiful tea set—just like this one! It was passed down from my great-grandmother. It holds a lot of family stories. It makes every tea time feel like a connection to my roots."

Ishiki smiled, his heart warmed by Bibian's stories. "That's incredible. I love how even tea can carry family history," he reflected. "In Japan, tea plays a similar role. We have tea ceremonies that celebrate art and tradition."

As they continued discussing their cultures over steaming cups, discussing their families, Bibian began sharing specific tales from her hometown of Taipei. "You would love it there during the holidays! The markets overflow with festive foods, and the streets are beautifully lit up. There are also special pet-themed decorations on display—did you know that we celebrate the Year of the Dog in our lunar calendar? Such themes intertwine with holiday celebrations too!"

"Every place has its unique way of celebrating," Ishiki mused, enthralled by the way Bibian brought her experiences to life. "It's fascinating how we can take elements from culture and weave them into our celebrations."

"Exactly! The culinary adventures from each household tell us so much about the people and their origins," Bibian said, her excitement palpable. "Now, let me give you a taste of a few Christmas treats I've prepared! I made pineapple cakes and almond jelly. It's a sweet way to celebrate our friendship and the festive season."

As she retrieved the beautifully packaged treats from her small backpack adorned with pins from her travels, Ishiki felt a sense of gratitude wash over him. The pineapple cake, with its crumbly exterior and sweet filling, was a favorite of hers. Spurred by curiosity, he eagerly tried each one, savoring the uniqueness of the flavors. "These are amazing! Different from our traditional cakes, for sure," he admitted, experiencing the layers of sweetness dancing on his tongue.

"Just like our friendship, we blend flavors together!" Bibian chuckled, her playful banter lightening the mood.

After finishing their tea and treats, the two friends decided to take their conversation elsewhere. "How about we head to the Nakamozu train station?" Ishiki suggested, feeling inspired to explore the essence of Bibian's stories in a more vibrant setting. "We can find some booths with Christmas goodies and perhaps even discover more treats together!"

"Great idea! There's a festive market there today, right? I can't wait to see what they have!" Bibian replied, hopping to her feet, excitement radiating from her.

They both quickly gathered their coats and stepped into the crisp, winter air. Walking towards Nakamozu Station—the bustling hub filled with life and light—excitement bubbled in their chests, making the chilly weather feel almost insignificant.

Once they arrived, they were welcomed by the sights and sounds of festive cheer—a bustling Christmas market filled with booths showcasing an array of seasonal delights and artisanal crafts. "Look at all the decorations!" Bibian exclaimed, pointing toward a booth laden with sparkling ornaments and handmade crafts. "They're so beautifully made!"

"Let's explore! This is such a great opportunity to learn about local traditions as well," Ishiki added, already mesmerized by the vibrant atmosphere around him.

As they strolled through the market, they sampled various treats—everything from rich, creamy custard to sweet grilled fish cakes. "This reminds me of some of the street food we have back in Taipei!" Bibian exclaimed while savoring the taste of spring rolls.

They paused at another stall featuring roasted chestnuts, which filled the air with roasted flavors. "This is an absolute must during the winter! Chestnuts are often enjoyed around Christmas," Ishiki explained, recalling the cozy scenes from his childhood.

"What does that feel like? The warmth from your family during the holidays? I think that's the essence of why we celebrate," Bibian asked, her curiosity evident.

"It's comforting," Ishiki replied thoughtfully. "When we gather around meals, it's about reconnecting, sharing stories, and feeling the love that binds us. Even if the dishes change, that connection stays true."

As they explored further, Bibian led him to a corner booth that caught her eye. "I have to try this! They have bubble tea! It's a Taiwanese classic, and I can't believe they're featuring it here!"

"I've heard of bubble tea but never tried it," Ishiki admitted, intrigued. In Taiwan, he knew it was much adored, often sipped alongside school life and social gatherings.

"Let's get a couple! You'll love the chewy tapioca pearls. Trust me!" she declared, her infectious enthusiasm prompting Ishiki to smile.

They ordered the unique drink, and as they made their way to a small table outside, Bibian took a sip and sighed, her eyes lighting up. "Ahhhh, bliss! Just like home." She offered him the cup after taking a sip.

"Okay, here goes! I'll try it," Ishiki said playfully, watching her encouragement intensify his courage. He took a careful sip, the flavors bursting with sweetness as the tapioca pearls danced on his tongue. "Wow! This is really fun!"

Bibian laughed, her joy radiating warmth amidst the chilly day. "I told you it would be! It's such a great treat to share with friends."

As they sat sipping their bubble tea, the bustle of the market around them felt vibrant, full of laughter and joy that seemed to echo the spirit of their friendship. They exchanged tales of their experiences, cultural quirks, and differences—each story blending seamlessly with the next.

"Why don't we create a new tradition?" Bibian suggested, her eyes glinting with excitement. "Let's write down all these moments we've enjoyed together and make them part of our Christmas story!"

Ishiki grinned at the idea. "That sounds beautiful! Our own version of a holiday book filled with memories fresh from our cultural experiences."

They decided to start drafting a "Cultural Christmas Journal," where they would each contribute reflections, memories, and recipes from their families. As they put their thoughts on paper, the act of blending their cultures transformed the day into a cherished creation—and a new tradition was born.

As they explored Nakamozu Market, their laughter intertwined with chatter, and the stories continued to flow as easily as the tea they had enjoyed earlier. When darkness began to blanket the market in a cozy embrace, lights twinkled overhead, casting a magical glow over the bustling crowds.

"Let's wrap up our day with a karaoke session! I bet we could sing a few tunes that celebrate our cultures," Bibian suggested, her vibrant spirit igniting their shared enthusiasm.

Ishiki laughed at the prospect. "Perfect! It's been a day of blending, so why not continue that theme with our music?"

With smiles on their faces and a new cultural tradition budding, they headed toward the cozy karaoke box that awaited them, already envisioning the laughter and joy that awaited as they celebrated the blending of their traditions—not just in food and stories, but in song and shared experiences too.

It felt as though their hearts resonated together, creating a harmony that echoed well beyond the notes they would soon sing—an appreciation for each other's cultures that would enrich their lives, forging a deeper bond that would resonate long after the Christmas lights dimmed. They reached the karaoke box, excitement bubbling over —with each song sung and each laugh shared, they knew this was just the beginning of their remarkable journey of cultural fusion and friendship.

CHAPTER 10: THE HOLIDAY'S DUAL NATURE

As the warm colors of dawn crept through Ishiki Nakamura's window, he stirred awake, eager for the day ahead. It was two days before Christmas, and the anticipation hung heavy in the air. Each day brought him closer to the gathering with Bibian, Yuki, Akira, and their other friends—a celebration they had all been eagerly preparing for. The mix of different cultures, stories, and traditions infused him with a sense of joy and excitement.

Ishiki slipped out of bed and made his way to the kitchen, where he could smell the aroma of freshly brewed coffee drifting into the air, a savored ritual he'd begun his mornings with since Bibian had arrived in Japan. He felt particularly grateful for these moments, a quiet time to reflect on how beautifully intertwined his life had become with Bibian's vibrant energy and the seamless blend of their cultures.

As he poured a cup, he glanced at the calendar hanging on his wall. It was peppered with notes and little doodles, reminders of all the gatherings, events, and now— coupled with his reflections from his earlier discussions with Bibian—notes about how the holiday season had evolved across cultures. His thoughts danced between the contrasting images of a chilly Christmas in Tokyo and the festive warmth of Bibian's Taiwanese celebrations, creating a rich tapestry of memories in his mind.

The doorbell chimed, breaking his reverie. "I'll get it," he called out, knowing it would likely be Bibian, who frequently visited to finalize the last details for their upcoming celebration. Sure enough, when he opened the door, her exuberant smile greeted him, her hair tied back in a playful ponytail, adorned with an array of colorful pins representing her travels.

"Good morning, Ishiki! I hope you're ready for some festive fun—today's the day we finalize all the decorations!" She bounced on her toes, her cheerful spirit radiating through the chilly morning air.

"Absolutely! I was just thinking about how amazing it is to blend our holiday traditions. Come in and grab a coffee!" he urged, stepping aside to let her in.

As she entered, the warmth of the apartment seemed to melt away the cold outside. They settled into the cozy living room adorned with seasonal decorations—paper ornaments crafted from colorful cardstock, fairy lights twinkling softly, and a small Christmas tree nestled in the corner wrapped in their collective memories.

While Ishiki set about preparing a couple more cups of coffee, Bibian gathered their decorations from three separate boxes filled with a variety of items she had collected during her time in Japan. "I brought some traditional Taiwanese decorations to mix in as well! I can't wait to show you!" she said excitedly, her hands rifling through the brightly colored pieces.

"Like what?" Ishiki asked, intrigued by the possibilities.

"Like these!" Bibian produced a set of brightly colored paper cutouts shaped like stars and lanterns, each one embodying the unique artistry of her hometown. "In Taiwan, we often decorate with these to symbolize hope and prosperity."

Ishiki examined the decorations with interest, admiring the intricate designs. "They're beautiful! They would look amazing next to our Japanese ornaments," he said. "We'll create a display that tells a story of both our cultures!"

Together, they spent the morning stringing lights and hanging decorations. Each ornament they placed seemed to capture the essence of their growing friendship, a beautiful amalgamation of traditions. As they worked, they chatted about their individual Christmas experiences.

"In Taiwan, even though Christmas isn't a public holiday, families make an effort to celebrate it in their own way," Bibian shared as she adjusted a lantern next to the tree. "We would gather for a feast, singing Christmas carols—even if they were Taiwanese versions! It's more about sharing the warmth of family rather than being about gifts and presents."

"That's similar to how it is in Japan. We often celebrate more with friends than family," Ishiki responded, putting the finishing touches on their decorations. "It's a blend of the Western holiday spirit with our unique flavors—fried chicken for dinner, of course!"

Bibian laughed, her eyes sparkling. "Yes! And the cakes, too. I'm so excited to see everyone's faces when they get a taste of our fusion cake!"

Once they finished decorating, the room radiated with warmth. The flickering lights cast playful shadows, while Bibian's colorful ornaments added a vibrant flair. They stepped back to admire their handiwork.

"I think we've created something special here," Ishiki said, a smile playing on his lips. "This reflects our journey together and the essence of our cultures."

"Exactly! Let's snap a picture to remember this moment," Bibian suggested, pulling out her phone. They gathered together in front of the tree, beaming, as she clicked the shutter.

Moments later, with a satisfied sigh, Bibian said, "Alright! What's next on our agenda?"

"Let's head to Nakamozu Station to pick up some festive snacks and drinks. The market should have some seasonal treats we can enjoy while we prepare for the gathering," Ishiki replied, excitement bubbling within him at the thought of sharing this cultural experience with their friends.

As they made their way to Nakamozu Station, the lively atmosphere enveloped them. They walked through throngs of people carrying shopping bags adorned with holly and bright red ribbons, the spirit of Christmas evident everywhere. Vendors lined the streets, offering everything from steaming cups of hot cocoa to sweet pastries, each stand filled with delights that echoed the season.

"I want to try the sweet potato balls! I've heard they're a must during the winter," Bibian exclaimed, tugging Ishiki toward a nearby stall where the vendor was serving something wrapped in crispy golden batter.

As they sampled the sweet potato delicacy, the warm flavors enveloped them like a cozy hug. "This is so good! It reminds me of a dessert we have during the Lunar New Year!" Bibian remarked, her eyes lighting up at the memories associated with the treat.

They continued exploring, sampling everything from Japanese dango to Taiwanese bubble tea, each bite further bridging the gap between their cultures. With each snack and sip, they learned about how holiday foods were not just meant to be consumed but savored, carrying stories of family gatherings and cherished memories.

"This is what I love about festivals—how they bring people together through food," Ishiki said, pausing long enough to look at Bibian. "So much of our identity is tied to what we eat during the holidays."

"Absolutely! Whether it's a fried chicken feast in Japan or hot pot in Taiwan, it speaks to our experiences," Bibian agreed, nodding enthusiastically.

As they navigated the bustling market, they spotted Akira and Yuki making their way toward them, their bright smiles shining through the crowd. "Hey, you two! Just in time to join the culinary journey!" Yuki exclaimed, her pastel ensemble a burst of happiness against the backdrop of the crowded market.

"Did you find any goodies yet?" Akira asked, glancing at the plates in their hands.

"Just sweet potato balls and bubble tea! We're on a quest for seasonal snacks to bring back for the gathering," Ishiki replied, gesturing for them to follow.

"I have some savory treats we can add," Akira said, leading the group toward a stall selling steaming slices of kurikinton, a sweet chestnut paste formed into small dumplings.

With their newfound snacking selections, they wandered the market before finally finding a charming little bakery, its glass case filled with an array of festive pastries. "This is the place!" Yuki exclaimed, pulling them in. "We need some special cakes for our gathering."

Bibian's eyes widened as she pointed excitedly at a display of dainty cakes topped with vibrant icing and seasonal fruits. "Look at those! They're gorgeous!"

They selected a few delectable pastries, discussing with the baker about the variety —a beautiful medley of flavors including matcha, mango, and red bean. With their arms laden with delicious treats, they stepped outside into the crisp winter air, their laughter blending seamlessly with the bustling sounds of the market.

"Let's head back and start our preparations! The sun will set soon, and we have to get everything ready before the gathering starts," Yuki said, her excitement taking the lead as they trod back toward Ishiki's apartment.

Once they arrived, the group fell into a comfortable rhythm of preparation—each person bringing their unique skills to the table. Bibian and Yuki began arranging the cakes and pastries on the table, while Akira and Ishiki set up the karaoke machine in the corner, a symphony of laughter accompanying each little task.

"Alright! Who's ready to rehearse our karaoke set?" Bibian called, clapping her hands together as the excitement in the room mounted.

They formulated a lineup, mixing traditional holiday songs from both cultures interspersed with modern pop hits—blending their identities beautifully in rhythm. Akira took the role of host, crafting a well-balanced setlist that assured everyone felt included in the melodic celebration.

As they practiced, a rich sense of camaraderie filled the room. They made memories with each note sung, the festive spirit amplifying their shared laughter. Ishiki felt proud as the duality of their cultures was woven into every song—it was a growing tapestry of friendship and understanding.

Later, as the evening approached, they opted for a break, gathering in the living room to enjoy a hot pot-style dinner—a nod to Taiwan's festive gatherings. Bibian had prepared an assortment of fresh vegetables, fish, and noodles. Akira and Yuki helped set the table, while Ishiki marveled at how beautifully this evening was unfolding.

As the hot pot simmered, they bantered about their favorite songs and shared holiday stories, creating a vibrant atmosphere reminiscent of a family gathering. "You know, for an occasion that originated in the West, Christmas has transformed into something that resonates deeply with our traditions," Akira remarked, raising his glass of warm sake.

Bibian nodded thoughtfully, her gaze drifting to the decorated tree. "This makes me realize that while each culture may have its unique way of celebrating, the essence of these gatherings—love, family, friendship—remains the same," she said softly.

Ishiki added, "Exactly! It's amazing how we get to learn from one another while creating our own traditions. I cherish each moment we share together."

"When we sing, decorate, and eat, we build these incredible memories that connect our cultures. The holiday really showcases the dual nature of Christmas—where all traditions can coalesce," Yuki chimed in.

Once dinner was prepared, they gathered around the table, overlooking a beautiful spread of steaming dishes. Each bite was not just a meal; it was a celebration and an intermingling of their unique heritages.

After dinner, it was finally time for their karaoke session. Each friend took a turn wielding the mic, singing their favorite songs from their respective cultures. Bibian performed a popular Taiwanese tune, her bright voice ringing through the cozy space, and Yuki followed suit with a beloved Japanese ballad, her sweet timbre captivating everyone.

"Okay, Ishiki, your turn!" Bibian cheered, handing him the microphone.

With a mix of nervousness and excitement, Ishiki stepped forward, his heart racing. He decided to sing a classic Japanese Christmas song that encapsulated the spirit of the season. As he sang, the warmth in the room felt palpable—a shared experience rich in laughter and memories.

As the night continued with harmonies intertwining, Bibian was struck with another idea. "Why don't we share one new tradition each Christmas, something that blends our cultures?" she suggested, looking around at her friends.

"I love that idea!" Yuki responded joyfully. "It could be anything—from food to music to how we decorate!"

Akira nodded in agreement, adding, "It would keep our gatherings fresh and exciting. Each holiday can be a new chapter in our shared story."

"I think we just created a new tradition," Ishiki said, smiling at the incredible bond forming around him.

As they wrapped up their karaoke night, the laughter and joy overflowed, filling the room with warmth. Each friend shared their favorites from the evening, reminiscing as they savored the unique tastes and songs that defined their extraordinary gathering.

When it was finally time to call it a night, they all agreed: the dual nature of the holiday—the merging of Taiwanese and Japanese traditions—had forged memories that would last a lifetime, expanding their connections beyond the boundaries of culture, growing into a family bound by love and laughter.

With Christmas just around the corner, they exited Ishiki's apartment with hearts full of promise, eager for the bustling days ahead that awaited them, ready to celebrate not only the holiday but the togetherness they had created along the way. Each commitment to one another formed a thread that would contribute to their rich tapestry of experiences—a joyful testament to the beautiful fusion of cultures, families, and lifelong friendships.

CHAPTER 11: GIFTS OF SWEETS AND SMILES

As the sun began to rise on the morning of Christmas Eve, the snow outside was gently falling, painting Ishiki Nakamura's apartment in a serene blanket of white. The atmosphere was imbued with warmth, echoing the melodies of laughter, bright memories, and shared stories that lingered from the previous night. Ishiki stretched in his bed, excitement bubbling within him as he thought of the day's plans. Today was the day they would navigate the gifts and sweets culture, exchanging delicious pastries and creating cherished memories together.

He rolled out of bed, pulling his edges of his curtains to reveal the beauty outside. The world looked beautifully still, a perfect canvas for the festivities to unfold. He made his way to the kitchen, the smell of tangy grapefruit tea that he brewed the night before filling the room as he heated it on the stove again. The warmth encouraged him to think about the joyful gathering he, Bibian, Yuki, and Akira had envisioned, one that would not just celebrate their friendship but also their intertwined cultures.

After a quick shower, Ishiki slipped on his favorite pair of jeans and a cozy hoodie before rearranging the decorations that could use a little bit of tidy-up for the gathering. With the holiday spirit enveloping him, he glanced around his living room, recalling all the fun they had decoratively blending their cultures.

Soon, the doorbell chimed cheerfully, breakng his focus on holiday decorations. "Coming!" he called, striding toward the door, his heart quickening at the thought of what Bibian could be bringing today.

"Happy Christmas Eve!" Bibian greeted him, her energy electrifying the air. She stood there, petite and vivacious, decked out in a playful red scarf and a stylish winter jacket that matched her colorfully decorated backpack. "I couldn't wait to see you!"

"Happy Christmas Eve! Come in!" Ishiki stepped aside, beaming at her infectious enthusiasm. His gaze was drawn to a small bag she was carrying, decorated with whimsical designs, presumably filled with goodies.

"I brought something really special!" Bibian declared as she stepped into the warmth of his apartment, shaking off the snowflakes that had settled in her hair. "Gifts and sweets for our gathering! I hope you're ready to dive into some deliciousness! I even made traditional Taiwanese pineapple cakes!"

"Oh wow! You know how much I love those." Ishiki's eyes widened in anticipation as she pulled out an intricately wrapped box. The familiar smell of buttery pastry wafted toward him, mingling perfectly with the grapefruit tea aroma. "You made them yourself?"

"Of course! It's a tradition that represents good fortune," Bibian replied with a proud grin. "Tonight, we can discuss what each of our sweets means in our culture."

His heart warmed at the thought. "That sounds wonderful! I've been wanting to learn more about the significance behind our holiday treats."

"In that case, we need to head to the bakery as well! Yuki and Akira will be there soon, and I want to pick up a few more traditional Japanese sweets to share," Bibian suggested enthusiastically, shouldering her bag again. "Oh, and don't forget the gifts we plan to exchange later!"

"Great idea! Let me pour us some tea, and we can head out," Ishiki chimed, feeling the comforting anticipation wrapping around him as if it were the Christmas lights adorning their homes.

As Bibian settled at the kitchen table to savor the pineapple cakes she had prepared, Ishiki carefully poured the warm grapefruit tea into two mugs, letting the tangy aroma fill the air. "This is delicious!" Bibian exclaimed after taking a bite, her eyes sparkling. "I can see why you love it!"

Once their tea ritual was complete, Ishiki and Bibian set off, walking hand in hand through the softly falling snowflakes toward the local Japanese bakery, a few blocks from his apartment. Nakamozu Station buzzed with early holiday shoppers, the aromas of freshly baked bread, pastries, and roasted chestnuts wafting invitingly through the icy air.

"Look at the decorations here! It's so festive!" Bibian proclaimed, her eyes dancing as every corner they turned revealed another twinkling light display. Nearby, children giggled while building snowmen, their laughter ringing like the joyful music playing through the streets.

"Oh, we need to take a picture here for our memories!" Ishiki suggested, pointing to a massive snowman wearing a comically large Santa hat standing by a fountain. He spotted a family nearby that seemed willing to capture their joyous moment on camera.

As they posed, shivering and laughing in the cold, Ishiki felt a rush of gratitude to have Bibian in his life, bridging the connection between their cultures seamlessly and making each moment meaningful.

Just before reaching the bakery's entrance, they saw Yuki and Akira walking toward them, clearly eager to join the festivities. Yuki wore a beautiful pastel coat cinched at the waist with a colorful scarf, her cheeks flushed from the cold. Akira looked dapper in a tailored jacket, his calm demeanor radiating warmth in the chilly air.

"Good morning! Happy Christmas Eve!" Yuki greeted as they arrived, her smile brightening their surroundings. "I've been thinking about our gathering tonight all day! Did Bibian share her goodies with you yet?"

"She was just telling me about her pineapple cakes," Ishiki replied, feeling the sense of joy swell within him as he observed their camaraderie. "We're on our way to the bakery to get some Japanese treats for everyone!"

"I have our Japanese Christmas cake order all set! I'm really excited to see everyone's reactions! I hope the bakery has the right ones for us," Yuki added as they entered the bakery, the warmth inside enveloping them like a hug. The space was adorned with colorful holiday decorations, and the counter was lined with an array of confectioneries.

As they huddled around the display case, the vibrant cakes and pastries braided with decorative elements showed a blend of Japanese and Western influences. "Look at those matcha and strawberry shortcakes! They're stunning!" Bibian exclaimed with delight, her hands clasped together as she pointed toward the colorful creations.

"Hmmm, we should also try 'kurian-masuto.' It's soft and natural chestnut flavored, perfect for the season!" Akira suggested thoughtfully, as he gingerly perused the options behind the counter.

"Let's ask for a mix of everything on display!" Yuki proposed, her enthusiasm infectious. The baker behind the counter, a kind woman with a warm smile, stepped forward to assist.

They enthusiastically shared their choices with her—the synergy of cultures reflected in their selections, intertwining together a blend of rich flavors and textures. After finalizing their order, they all huddled together as the baker packed their goodies into festive boxes.

With warm treats in hand and grins brightening their faces, the friends decided to take a short detour on their way back. "Let's grab some seasonal drinks from the café down the street!" Bibian exclaimed, her excitement spilling over. "I want you all to try the winter-exclusive matcha latte!"

"I've had it once! It's an absolute must when it gets cold, and there's no better time for it than today," Ishiki nodded, already envisioning the comforting taste.

Once they reached the café, the warm air buzzed with the chatter of happy patrons seeking refuge from the cold. They ordered four steaming matcha lattes topped with frothy milk and delectable whipped cream. Settling into a comfortable corner table, they toasted their drinks, laughter and chatter filling the air.

"This is delicious! Thank you for suggesting it, Bibian!" Akira complimented, already on his second sip.

"I'm so glad you like it—this warmth is perfect for today!" Bibian's cheeks were rosy, her energy radiating around the table.

As their conversation flowed freely—discussing traditions and laughs, recipes and flavors—Bibian leaned forward suddenly, her voice filled with enthusiasm: "Say, do you all remember the stories behind our particular holiday sweets? What do they mean back in your homes?"

"What a great idea! I'd love to hear that—especially since we're going to be sharing them later!" Ishiki replied eagerly.

"Okay! I'll start with the pineapple cakes," Bibian said, her eyes shimmering with joy. "In Taiwan, these symbolize prosperity and good fortune. They are usually given as gifts. My family would exchange them with friends and neighbors during the holidays, spreading goodwill and cheer."

"That's lovely! The meanings adds so much depth," Yuki said, her heartwarming smile encouraging her friend to continue.

Ishiki took a moment, reflecting on his culture. "In Japan, our Christmas cakes—specifically the strawberry shortcakes—are often more about celebrating moments. We typically make them to commemorate special occasions, and as such, they represent joy and happiness. They're a way of sharing our good fortune and friendship, especially during this festive season."

"Now there's the kurian-masuto!" Akira interjected. "Like the winter chestnut cakes, they embody the warmth of home, a reflection of familial gatherings and warmth during Christmas. It's a dessert that showcases how we cherish these moments with families."

The air buzzed around them, the rich context of their treats simmering beautifully amongst the warmth and laughter echoing through the cozy café.

"I love all these connections we share through food. They truly create a tapestry of traditions," Bibian marveled, adjusting her ponytail, her bright eyes shining with appreciation.

"Exactly," Yuki chimed in, "it's like each dessert carries a piece of our culture, a representation of who we are. Now, tonight, we get to exchange our sweets and create new memories!"

"I can't wait to see everyone's reaction to our flavors and stories!" Ishiki said, brimming with enthusiasm.

As they finished up their drinks, whispers of excitement wove their way through their chatter. The thrill of anticipation for the evening festivities grew, as they imagined the winter wonderland they would be creating together, filled with laughter and warmth—hand-in-hand, every sweet moment one step closer to becoming a cherished memory.

When they concluded their drinks, the friends gathered their treats, making their way back to Ishiki's apartment, ready to set the stage for the cultural exchange and celebration that awaited.

As they entered the cozy living room, the warm glow from the fairy lights danced against the soft wall décor, setting the perfect backdrop for their festive gathering. Bibian placed the beautifully wrapped pineapple cakes on the table while Yuki carefully arranged the colorful pastries. Akira shared the chestnut cake with reverent care, clearly excited to introduce everyone to its significance.

With smiles shining brightly on their faces, the four friends leaned into these shared moments as they prepared to make new traditions.

As they decorated their gathering table together, Bibian's excitement bubbled forth. "Who will lead our gift exchange?"

"I can't wait to see everyone's faces when they unwrap their gifts!" Ishiki said, his heart beating faster.

"Let me take the lead," Yuki said, her gentle demeanor radiating warmth. She placed festive decorations around the table, creating an inviting atmosphere.

As the sun set and the room began to glow with the soft light of candles, they each took turns, carefully exchanging gifts and sweets. Laughter filled the air as they unwrapped thoughtfully chosen items—a small karaoke microphone for Ishiki, a vibrant tea set for Bibian—the significance of each heartfelt gift deepening the bond between them.

Once the last gift was opened, they paused momentarily, gazing at each other before bursting into spontaneous laughter.

"This has been such a beautiful day, filled with sweetness and smiles," Akira remarked, taking a moment to appreciate the gathering before them.

"Let's raise a toast! To friendship, to sweet traditions, and to the beautiful blending of our cultures!" Bibian announced, her voice full of joy.

They clinked their mugs together, celebrating not only the sweetness in their treats but the joy that filled the room—an embodiment of their new traditions, echoing through the festivities and hearts alike. This Christmas Eve would surely be marked in their memory, an indelible mark of connection—increasing the warmth in their friendships with every exchange of sweets and smiles.

CHAPTER 12: KARAOKE DREAMS AND MEMORIES

As Ishiki Nakamura adjusted the settings on the karaoke machine, a kaleidoscope of vibrant lights flickered around the cozy karaoke box, the air thick with palpable excitement. Bibian stood nearby, clutching the remote in one hand and a sparkling microphone in the other, bouncing lightly on her toes.

"Ready, ready!" she beamed, the joy radiating from her face as she beheld the colorful display. The soft hum of a familiar melody began filling the room, a cheerful mix that complemented the vibrant atmosphere perfectly. Ishiki chuckled at her infectious energy, feeling the warmth of friendship envelop him like a soft blanket.

"Let's kick this off with a classic!" Ishiki suggested, his voice brimming with enthusiasm as he flipped through the list of songs. His fingers ran over the familiar titles until he landed on a beloved Japanese holiday song, one that had been a staple in his family celebrations.

"Have you ever heard of 'Kurisumasu ni wa Kuri no Kaibutsu'? It's about the special moments we share during Christmas," he explained, the nostalgic tune bringing a wave of warmth and recollection to his heart.

"I haven't! But it sounds wonderful! Let's sing it," Bibian replied, her long black hair glinting under the bright lights as she leaned closer, her eyes sparkling with excitement.

With a deep breath, Ishiki stepped up to the microphone, the moment feeling significant like he was about to weave a story into the very fabric of their memories. He started singing, his voice echoing off the soundproof walls, bringing the song to life. The melody mixed with the warmth of the cozy space, and as he sang, thoughts of family gatherings and past celebrations enveloped him.

Bibian joined in, a mirthful smile spreading across her face as she harmonized with him, her spirit infusing the moment with joy. Their voices intertwined, dancing gracefully around the lyrics as they celebrated their cultures through music, each note ringing out like a testament to their friendship and shared experiences.

After completing the song, they burst into laughter, the thrilling atmosphere tinged with elation. Ishiki's cheeks were flushed with excitement, and he looked over at Bibian, her enthusiasm contagious. "That was amazing! Your voice adds so much life to the song!"

"Thank you! But I think we really captured the spirit together," she replied, her mischief peeking through. "Now, what's next? I think it's time for you to try one of my favorites!"

Without waiting for an answer, she swiftly scrolled through the list, her eyes narrowing in concentration before settling on a lively pop tune from Taiwan. "This one will get everyone up and dancing! Are you ready to be a superstar, Ishiki?"

"Only if you livestream it!" he joked, but his heart raced as he felt her determination push him forward. When she pressed the play button, the catchy beat infused the room with energy, and Bibian threw herself into the performance, her expressive movements capturing the heart of the song.

Ishiki laughed but soon found himself swept away by the infectious rhythm, letting the music move him as he joined her. Despite his initial hesitation, he danced and sang with abandon, the lyrics flowing through him. The moment symbolized their growing friendship—a blend of cultures, laughter, and encouragement.

As they danced, Akira and Yuki entered the karaoke box, vibrant smiles gracing their faces, igniting the energy in the room even further. "What's happening in here?" Akira called out, raising his eyebrow playfully as he stepped in.

"Just a superstar performance! Join us!" Bibian beckoned, extending her hand, inviting them into the whirlwind of music and laughter.

Yuki stepped forward, her cheerful expression lighting the dimmed space. "What's next on the lineup? We can't miss out on this fun!"

"Let's do a duet!" Ishiki suggested, the idea bubbling with excitement in his chest. "Bibian and I have just finished singing a Taiwanese hit, so maybe we can mix it up and sing a traditional holiday song next!"

"Perfect! I've been wanting to try 'Seiko Matsuda's 'Furusato'! It brings such warm feelings of home," Yuki said, her cheeks brightening as she took the microphone from Bibian.

"Great choice!" Akira chimed in, taking a seat while observing eagerly. The room buzzed with anticipation as Yuki began the song, her voice gently weaving a story about nostalgia and belonging, resonating deeply with their hearts.

As she sang, Ishiki fell into an introspective state, surrounded by close friends and cherished memories. The essence of their cultures resonated wonderfully in the atmosphere, each note enveloping them with warmth as they celebrated their different backgrounds. In that moment, he felt a deep understanding of how intertwined their lives had become, not just through songs but through the experiences they had shared throughout the season.

Bibian chimed in with harmonies, lifting Yuki's voice even higher, creating an otherworldly blend. Ishiki's heart swelled at the beauty of it all—their musical journey reaching beyond the confines of the karaoke box, intertwining their legacy of friendship.

When the song concluded, the room erupted in applause, a symphony of happy cheers and laughter that echoed off the walls. "That was stunning!" Ishiki exclaimed, watching Yuki's cheeks flush with gratification.

"You two made it special! Let's do more!" Akira encouraged, his calm demeanor a contrast to the lively energy buzzing in the room.

They took turns choosing songs, with many shifting between traditional anthems and popular hits, creating a delightful fusion of cultures. Each time Bibian picked a

Taiwanese song, she passionately described its significance and her memories associated with it, deepening their connection to the music and to her background.

"I remember singing this song while sharing bubble tea with friends in Taipei," she reminisced as the beat dropped, infectious laughter pooling among them. "We'd gather in parks, enjoying the ambiance while capturing moments together—just like this!"

Her words painted a vivid picture, and as they sang along with her, they felt the essence of those moments slipping through time. The connections they forged through stories and music blossomed beautifully.

"Ishiki, I think you need to try singing a famous J-pop song next! Something everyone knows!" Bibian suggested, her eyes gleaming with mischief.

"Okay, but you have to join me for the chorus!" he replied, the thought of sharing the stage with his friends buzzing in his mind. They settled on a popular song that had transcended cultures—a harmonious anthem of unity.

As Ishiki's vocal notes filled the air, the lights flickering rhythmically in tune, it was as if each chord drew them closer together in shared memories and laughter. Bibian's vibrant energy matched his, her voice shooting up to meet the high notes, bringing their melodies together seamlessly.

After their performance, Yuki spurred the group to switch gears. "Okay! It's time for a group song! Something classic that merges both cultures!"

"Like 'We Are the World'? It speaks about coming together, which fits beautifully with our friendship!" Akira suggested, his voice laced with sincerity.

"That's wonderful! How about the four of us take turns for verses while singing the chorus together?" Bibian agreed, her enthusiasm spurring everyone on.

As they began, each voice contributed a layer of warmth that enveloped the room. They took turns, weaving personal contributions in a chorus of harmony—every line reflecting their shared experiences, dreams, and the connections they cherished.

When they reached the final line, a beautiful silence hung in the air—a moment to soak in what they had created together. It was magical; the shared energy turned into a wonderful memory, a cornerstone of their friendship immortalized through song.

In the aftermath of their last song, laughter intertwined with memories as they began recounting their most treasured moments of the night. Each anecdote brought forth fond smiles, a cohesive blend of cultures echoing through their joyful connection.

"Let's not let tonight be our last karaoke fest—I want this to be a tradition!" Yuki declared, her excitement beaming brightly. "Let's gather each season and mix traditional songs from our homes—our own 'Karaoke of Cultures'!"

"I love that idea!" Ishiki replied, his heart swelling with affection for the bond they had built. "Each gathering can tell a different story, bring us closer as friends!"

As the night wore on, they shared their experiences of what Christmas meant in their cultures, performance melding with heartfelt conversation. Their laughter resonated, an affirmation of the beautifully shared friendship they were cultivating—a unique blend stitched together through music and camaraderie.

Once it felt like the time to wind down, they started wrapping up their singing. Ishiki enjoyed the buzz of contentment coursing through him, enriched by a evening of beautiful harmonies. He stole glances at Bibian and his friends, feeling grateful for the collective experiences shared—they had not only dived deep into each other's cultures but had continued to nurture a blossoming friendship that was as warm and comforting as the holiday season itself.

"Alright, this has been a magical night!" Ishiki announced, his voice sincere as the others nodded, bemused smiles adorning their faces. "But let's hold onto this energy and carry it into tomorrow's adventures!"

Before stepping out into the cool winter night, they shared a final group hug—a unified celebration of their bond, a culmination of shared songs and stories. As they exited the karaoke box, the lively colors faded into their memories, leaving them to cherish the moments they had built together.

In the quiet of the evening streets, surrounded by the festive glow, they knew their journey had only just begun. Each encounter intertwined through laughter and creativity would lead them into the future, sculpting a friendship that promised to shine brightly, filled with the dreams, songs, and memories that awaited them. And as they walked, hearts light with joy and companionship, they felt the spirit of Christmas enfolding them—echoing the essence of togetherness they were meant to celebrate this year and every year to come.

CHAPTER 13: CULTURAL CURIOSITIES UNVEILED

As Christmas Day dawned quietly over Nakamozu, the soft light filtering through Ishiki Nakamura's window cast a golden hue over the cozy apartment. The world outside was enshrouded in a gentle layer of pristine snow, lending an air of serenity to the bustling excitement brewing within. It was a day filled with promise, where young hearts swirled with anticipation for the festivities that awaited them.

Ishiki's heart raced as he made his way to the kitchen, the aroma of brewed coffee intricately intertwining with the sweetness of leftover pastries from their gathering the previous night. The warm glow of the fairy lights continued to flicker cheerfully, remnants from their decorations setting the perfect holiday ambiance.

Today would not only be about exchanging gifts and good cheer but also about unveiling the cultural curiosities that each of them brought to the gathering. Ishiki looked forward to exploring deeper conversations about heritage and how these influences shaped their identities.

The doorbell chimed, pulling him from his thoughts. "Coming!" he called, moving quickly toward the sound.

Opening the door revealed a petite figure sparkling with enthusiasm—Bibian Moon stood outside, bundled in a vibrant red coat, her cheeks rosy from the cold. Her small backpack was adorned with pins of various places, and she held a large box of goodies in her hands, an eager smile lighting her features.

"Good morning, Ishiki! Merry Christmas!" Bibian exclaimed, her voice effervescent. "I brought special Taiwanese treats to share with everyone!"

"Good morning, Bibian! Merry Christmas to you too!" Ishiki replied joyfully, stepping aside. "What treats did you bring?"

Bibian opened the box to reveal beautifully arranged pineapple cakes, almond crisps, and colorful chewy candies. "I couldn't resist bringing a variety. I wanted to showcase a few more traditional flavors from Taiwan that represent the festive spirit!"

Ishiki's eyes widened in appreciation. "These look amazing! You always think of the best surprises. I can't wait to share them with everyone."

Just then, the door swung open again, and Akira Yamamoto and Yuki Tanaka entered, laughter spilling into the living room like a warm embrace. Both wore festive attire: Yuki in a pastel blue dress with reindeer patterns and Akira in a stylish blazer paired with a Christmas-themed tie. "Merry Christmas!" they chorused, their voices ringing in harmony with the holiday spirit.

"Merry Christmas, you two!" Ishiki and Bibian replied in unison, grinning at the sight of their friends brimming with holiday cheer.

"Yuki, did you bring those traditional Japanese snacks I asked you to?" Ishiki inquired, knowing how fond he was of the culinary delights of the season.

"Of course!" Yuki replied, frantically rummaging through her pastel-colored tote bag. "I brought an assortment of mochi, some taiyakis filled with sweet red bean paste, and a couple of Christmas cakes that I ordered from the local bakery."

As Yuki showcased the delicious array of snacks on the table, Ishiki glanced toward Akira, who was preparing to unveil a surprise of his own. "I have something relevant to share too, something I've been wanting to introduce to you guys as part of our gathering today," Akira announced, his voice calm yet spirited.

He reached into his bag and pulled out a beautifully wrapped book. "This is a collection of folktales from various regions in Japan. I thought it would be a fantastic way to blend our discussions about cultural curiosity and how stories shape our unique identities," he explained, handing the book to Ishiki.

"Oh wow! This is perfect!" Ishiki said, flipping open the cover. "We can share stories from both Taiwan and Japan, exploring our roots while also learning about each other's traditions."

"There's nothing that brings friends together quite like a good story," Yuki mused, her eyes sparkling with delight. "We should take turns reading—sharing tales about our cultures and backgrounds while enjoying all these delicious treats!"

Bibian nodded enthusiastically. "Let's start with some food and then dive into our stories. This is an opportunity for us to unveil curiosities and connect deeply through storytelling."

With everyone settled comfortably around the table, they began tasting the assortment of treats Bibian and Yuki had brought. Each delicious bite was met with joyful exclamations, the warm flavors resonating with their fond memories of family gatherings and celebrations.

"This pineapple cake has a texture that reminds me of a flaky pie crust, infused with sweet, tangy pineapple! It's incredible!" Ishiki marveled, savoring the taste.

Bibian beamed. "I am so glad you like it! With every bite, I hope it brings a sense of good fortune to our celebration. In Taiwan, we eat these during the New Year—they represent prosperity and joy!"

"I think I'll have to add some to my New Year's traditions too!" Ishiki smiled as he took another one, eager to learn more about Bibian's cultural significance of these treats.

Yuki chimed in, "Speaking of traditions, I can't wait to try these mochi! May I??" She held out a fluffy piece covered in soybean flour, her excitement palpable.

"Yes, and those taiyakis are a must for this holiday. They're always filled with sweet surprises, much like this gathering!" Ishiki grinned, watching as Yuki indulged in the assortment of foods they had driven together, capturing the essence of their cultures in every delectable morsel.

Once they finished their kitchen feast, the table gleamed with delightful empty plates, a testament to their joviality shared through food. "Shall we begin our storytelling session?" Akira suggested, leaning comfortably into his chair, passing the folktale book to Bibian.

Bibian opened the book carefully, flipping through the pages filled with vibrant illustrations and enchanting tales. "I'll start with a story that has always resonated with me, something that highlights the importance of family and values during the festive season," she said warmly, clearing her throat.

As she began reading, her voice carried the narrative like a subtle melody, weaving an intricate tapestry of familial bonds and the spirit of giving. The story spoke of a humble family living in Taiwan, preparing for the New Year, highlighting their kindness and tradition. With each word, she drew her friends into a world of cultural richness—an invitation into her homeland.

When she finished, Yuki's eyes sparkled with fascination. "That was beautiful, Bibian. It makes me realize how interconnected and universal our values are, regardless of where we come from."

Ishiki smiled, his heart swelling with gratitude for creating this intimate space of shared stories. "It also demonstrates that culture shapes who we are and the values we hold dear. I'd love to share a tale from my home next," he offered, flipping through the pages to find a story that captured his sentiments perfectly.

As he read, his story unfolded like a vivid painting—the vibrant colors of each character and their journey resonating seamlessly with his experiences, giving life to the essence of Japanese tradition. It revolved around the celebration of traditional festivals and the importance of remembering one's heritage, anchoring the narrative in a backdrop of warmth and togetherness.

After every story, they all shared reflections, offering insights and deeper connections as tales bridged their backgrounds, and laughter echoed in harmonious undertones. They discovered how stories carved their identities—tying them to their personal experiences while weaving intricacies of culture into the fabric of their friendship.

After Ishiki's reading, Akira shared a story steeped in Japanese folklore that revealed the strength of community during times of hardship. His calm, grounding voice resonated through the quiet room, painting rich visuals that held everyone captive in a spell of fascination. The room thrummed with energy, filled with animated discussions that connected their experiences, enabling each character from the stories to come alive within the group.

Yuki followed suit, sharing a classic Japanese tale about perseverance and love. She spoke of the bond between a girl and her loyal dog, transcending time and distance, reminding everyone of their own cherished memories.

As they shared these curiosities—stories crafted through generations—they realized the profound influence of narratives within their lives. They celebrated how different cultural elements harmonized into a single journey, allowing them to delve deeper into their friendships while learning about each other's heritages.

"I think we should make this a tradition," Bibian said after a stirring silence, her eyes reflecting sincerity. "At every gathering, let's share new stories—whether through food, songs, or folktales. They hold memories, create connections, and ignite understanding."

"I couldn't agree more," Yuki added, visibly moved. "This is what makes our friendship stronger—a rich tapestry woven with threads of culture, laughter, and experiences."

Ishiki nodded fervently. "Absolutely! Each glimpse into our backgrounds not only enriches our identities but weaves us closer as friends. Tonight, our traditions blend beautifully—stories and food intertwine. It's such a precious time."

Feeling inspired, Akira suggested, "Perhaps we could even collaborate on a story that mixes our cultures together—each of us contributing a piece that reflects our experiences during the holidays!"

"That would be amazing!" Bibian exclaimed, her enthusiasm brightening the atmosphere.

As the night progressed, laughter mingled with shared stories, each moment reinforcing their friendship while expanding their understanding of one another's backgrounds. The warmth in the room felt palpable, bound by the shared narratives that interlocked gracefully, illuminating the foundation of their diverse experiences.

Eventually, they prepared to wrap up the evening, hearts filled with fond memories and laughter. They lingered a bit longer over the remaining treats, wanting to let the beauty of the night linger in the air just a little more.

"I can't wait for our next gathering. Let's keep the spirit alive and continue to explore our cultures through stories and food," Ishiki said sincerely, looking around at his friends.

"Here's to many more stories, adventures, and delicious treats!" Bibian raised her glass, echoing Ishiki's sentiments.

They clinked their glasses together, laughter echoing through Ishiki's cozy apartment, the Christmas lights twinkling like stars as memories of cherished friendships danced across their minds.

As they bid goodbye, the fading echoes of the night clung in the air—an indelible mark on their hearts, reminding them that the essence of togetherness transcended cultural boundaries, each experience a brushstroke painting the portrait of their friendship—a beautiful amalgamation of the curious, the joyous, and the rich tapestry of their lives woven together through the tales they shared. The night was more than just an exchange of cultures; it was a celebration of their lives, a mosaic illuminated by understanding, laughter, and, most importantly, love.

CHAPTER 14: NAVIGATING THE HOLIDAY RUSH

The morning after their celebratory gift exchange was once again draped in a soft layer of fresh snow. As Ishiki Nakamura gazed out his window, the world sparkled in icy brilliance, transforming the streets of Nakamozu into a winter wonderland. Today, the anticipation of Christmas felt even more palpable as it shimmered in the air, filled with both excitement and a hint of anxiety. The holiday rush was upon them, and the urge to create the perfect festive experience loomed large.

He shook off the lingering traces of sleep and prepared a quick breakfast, reminding himself that this day was as much about enjoying the little moments as it was about the preparations that lay ahead. He poured himself a cup of warm grapefruit tea, its comforting aroma weaving through his cozy kitchen, mixing perfectly with the festive remnants still lingering from the previous evening.

A sudden flurry of texts erupted on his phone, pulling him from his morning reverie. It was Bibian, her enthusiasm vibrant even through a screen. "Good morning, Ishiki! Are you ready for our big day? We need to get on the move soon if we want to beat the holiday rush at Nakamozu Station!"

With a chuckle, Ishiki replied, "Give me half an hour, and I'll be there! What's our first stop?"

"We're meeting Akira and Yuki to check on our ice skating plans and grab lunch at that new market!" Bibian texted back, her excitement translating in every word.

"I'll see you soon!" Ishiki responded, already feeling the rush of the day working its way into his veins. He quickly cleaned up and dressed in a comfortable outfit, snatching his warm hoodie and a pair of jeans before darting out the door.

The streets were buzzing, a lively mixture of bustling shoppers, families, and young couples, all eager to capture the magic of the season. Holiday music floated through the air, combining with the laughter and chatter of the crowd. He felt a thrill run through him—this vibrant atmosphere reflected the strength of community and shared celebration.

Upon arriving at Nakamozu Station, Ishiki spotted Bibian standing in front of the entrance, her black hair bouncing lightly as she waved him over. "Ishiki! Over here!" she called out, her bright scarf fluttering against the gentle breeze.

"Hey! You're looking festive!" Ishiki replied, noting the patterned warmth of her coat. "Ready to tackle the rush?"

"Absolutely! Let's go find Akira and Yuki before we lose them in this crowd!" She giggled, her eyes dancing with excitement as they stepped inside the station.

Moments later, Akira and Yuki joined them, both navigating the station with purpose. Akira's calm demeanor provided a reassuring presence amid the vibrant chaos, while Yuki's cheerful energy was contagious.

"Hello! We were just discussing the best route to the market," Yuki said, bouncing slightly on the balls of her feet. "There's supposed to be an amazing Christmas market with local artisans just a short walk away!"

"I've heard great things about it," Akira added, glancing at his watch. "We should head over quickly before the crowds become unmanageable. Let's make this a fun adventure!"

The group navigated through the station, filled with holiday shoppers hustling to find last-minute gifts. They squeezed past a few stalls selling seasonal ware, the vibrant colors of handmade crafts and decorations catching their eyes momentarily. Bibian stopped to admire delicate ornaments crafted in intricate detail.

"Maybe we can return later for some souvenirs?" she suggested, her enthusiasm illuminating her features.

"Definitely! But for now, let's stick to the plan," Ishiki encouraged, seamlessly leading them out of the station and onto the street where the sun shone brightly, glistening off the fresh snow.

As they walked, the laughter and chatter around them intertwined with the sounds of holiday music spilling from nearby shops. They moved confidently toward the market, delighted by the holiday decorations lining the pathway. The scent of caramel and roasted chestnuts wafted through the air, drawing their attention to a street vendor selling tempting treats.

"Wanna grab some roasted chestnuts for later?" Bibian asked, glancing at the vendor cheerfully cracking open warm, golden nuts.

"Sure! That sounds perfect," Ishiki replied instinctively, while Yuki nodded eagerly, realizing they could snack on those while exploring the market.

They purchased a bag and continued their stroll, the warm aroma accompanying them as they approached the bustling market. Upon arrival, they were greeted by a vibrant array of stalls, each showcasing artisanal foods, handmade crafts, and local delicacies.

"Look at that!" Yuki exclaimed, pointing toward a stall adorned with colorful knitted scarves and gloves. "Those would make adorable gifts for my family!"

"Good idea! Let's check out what else they have," Akira suggested, leading the way. As they moved from stall to stall, the friends found themselves drawn into lively conversations with enthusiastic vendors, each eager to share the stories behind their creations.

Bibian found herself entranced by a display of intricately designed ceramics, delicate and decorative tea sets that reminded her of home. "These are beautiful! I'd love to take one back to Taiwan as a memory," she murmured thoughtfully, her fingers tracing the rim of a dainty teacup.

Ishiki stepped up beside her, admiration in his voice. "They really are lovely. It'd be a perfect way to remember this trip and our time together."

After exploring a myriad of stalls, they decided to sample various foods from the market—a smorgasbord of flavors representing both local Japanese cuisine and international treats imbued with holiday flair. They devoured freshly made takoyaki, sizzling with flavor, and savored sweet mochi filled with red bean paste. Laughter erupted as they tried to capture the perfect picture of the group amidst all the culinary delights.

"Okay, one with the takoyaki!" Bibian called, balancing several skewers in her hands, her laughter infectious as they posed. Joyful memories were captured in snapshots and giggles, solidifying their day in the heart of the festive spirit.

"Let's head over to the ice rink now!" Akira suggested, glancing at his watch. "We've spent quite a bit of time here!"

The group agreed, navigating their way through the busy market crowds, the sounds of cheers intermingling with holiday tunes leading them to the nearby ice skating rink. Upon arrival, they were met with gleaming ice and a flurry of happy skaters twirling and soaring across the surface.

They secured their skates and embraced the excitement of gliding across the ice. Bibian took a moment to adjust, her petite frame wobbling at first as she took her first steps onto the rink. Ishiki skated beside her, offering encouragement. "You've got this! Just find your center!"

"Easier said than done!" she laughed, her cheeks flushed from the cold and exhilaration. As they navigated the rink, small victories filled their hearts, laughter spilling over as they encouraged each other.

Yuki took to the ice gracefully, following Akira's smooth movements as they glided hand-in-hand. "Why don't you join us, Bibian?" she called as they twirled in delight.

"I will! But only if I don't fall first!" Bibian exclaimed, shoving herself forward with joyful determination. With every push against the ice, she found her balance, laughter bubbling as she whirled around in delight.

Ishiki beamed at his friends, intoxicated by the sheer joy of the moment. They were all navigating their own challenges together—something that transformed the ice rink into a celebration of persistence and togetherness.

As they skated, Bibian broke into a joyful rendition of a classic winter song, her voice rising above the din, inviting her friends to join her. Then the laughter continued, increased to the highs of exuberant cheers each time any of them stumbled or spun wildly, leading to inevitable tumbles often followed by echoes of laughter.

"Maybe we can build a snowman once we're done ice skating?" Bibian suggested, her bright spirit lighting up the chilly afternoon.

"That sounds amazing! We could have a mini snowman contest!" Yuki added, her eyes sparkling as she contemplated the possibilities.

Akira nodded approvingly. "Let's do that! It'll be a fun way to cap off our day."

As the afternoon turned to early evening, they reluctantly took off their skates, hearts warmed with accomplishment and laughter ringing in their ears. "What a fantastic way to spend Christmas Eve! I never want this day to end," Ishiki said, his spirit warm with joy.

"Let's grab dinner at that cozy place around the corner that serves ramen," Yuki suggested, her stomach growling in agreement.

With renewed energy, they set out toward the restaurant, the excitement for dinner bubbling beneath their skin. The warm atmosphere of the ramen shop enveloped them as they entered, the intoxicating aroma of freshly cooked broth swirling around them, inviting them to indulge.

"I can almost taste it already!" Bibian cheered, her eyes bright with anticipation as they settled at a large table, sipping on cups of hot green tea while they chatted about their plans for Christmas day.

Over hearty bowls of steaming ramen, they exchanged stories about holiday memories from their respective cultures, weaving the day's adventures into their narrative tapestry. Each anecdote simmered with emotion, deepening their connections as they shared laughter seasoned with authenticity.

As the sun set and darkness fell outside, the shop came alive with soft lantern light that warmed the room. Bibian looked around, a content smile gracing her lips. "This has been the best day—I love how we all came together to celebrate our traditions!"

"I agree completely," Akira replied, nodding as he savored a final bite of ramen. "It's beautiful how we all bring our unique flavors into this friendship."

Ishiki couldn't help but feel grateful for every moment spent with his friends. The blend of cultures meshed together seamlessly, creating a harmony that highlighted the true spirit of the holiday season—the essence of togetherness, open hearts, and shared joy.

With the fulfilling taste of the day settling within them, they stepped back into the colder air, snow beginning to fall again softly around them as they made their way home. The sights of Nakamozu, twinkling with holiday lights, built a sense of nostalgia, painting vibrant memories across the backdrop of their shared adventures.

As they approached Ishiki's apartment, they exchanged warm hugs and festive wishes for the day ahead, anticipation swelling for the Christmas festivities, knowing these moments would create a beautiful tradition that celebrated the magic of friendship, culture, and collaboration.

"See you all bright and early tomorrow!" Ishiki called, watching their silhouettes turn to cheerful laughter as they waved goodbye, disappearing into the snowy streets.

Closing the door behind him, he absorbed the warmth of his surroundings, the remnants of the day mingling with the delightful scent of holiday treats still lingering in the air. Setting down his bag, Ishiki took a moment to reflect on the joyful chaos of the day. Navigating the holiday rush had been filled with tender memories, laughter, and most importantly, friendships that blazed against the winter chill, warming their spirits and fortifying their bonds for many seasons to come.

CHAPTER 15: THE SPLENDOR OF SEASONAL LIGHTS

In the heart of Nakamozu, the streets glimmered like a dream woven from stardust. The sun had dipped below the horizon, leaving a curtain of twilight over the city. A rush of cold air danced through the streets, invigorating Ishiki Nakamura as he pulled his hoodie tighter around him. He had been looking forward to this evening—the annual Winter Illumination Festival was finally here.

Ishiki stood outside his apartment, staring at the soft glow of the twinkling fairy lights that adorned the trees lining the street. He took a moment to appreciate the transformation of their ordinary neighborhood into a whimsical wonderland. Sparkling lights hung above him like stars, the colors reflecting off newly fallen snow, turning the world into a canvas of vibrant hues. He couldn't help but feel a tingle of excitement as he thought of the night ahead, the gathering of friends to witness the beauty together.

His phone buzzed, drawing him out of his reverie. A text from Bibian illuminated the screen: "Can't wait to see you! Where should we meet?"

A smile crept onto Ishiki's face as he typed back, "Let's meet at the fountain in the park! It's the best spot for the lights." He knew the fountain, encircled by glowing orbs, would serve as a perfect backdrop for the festivities.

"Great! See you soon! 🎇" Bibian replied almost instantly.

As Ishiki made his way to the park, he passed the local bakery, the scent of freshly baked goods wafting through the air. He couldn't resist stepping inside for a moment, enamored by the festive decorations inside the quaint shop. A beautiful array of Christmas cakes and pastries was displayed under twinkling lights, and he decided to indulge in a couple of sweet treats to share with his friends later.

"Good evening, Ishiki!" the baker greeted, his jovial voice bringing warmth to the shop. "Trying to get in the festive spirit? We have a new spiced chestnut cake if you're interested!"

"That sounds delightful! I'll take two of those, please," Ishiki replied, envisioning how happy his friends would be to share in the treat.

After purchasing the cakes, he tucked them safely into his backpack and hurried toward the park nestled in the heart of Nakamozu. The park was already bustling with families and couples, their laughter mixing with the melodic sounds of distant carolers.

Upon arriving at the fountain, Ishiki spotted Bibian bouncing on her toes, her cheerful energy illuminating the chilly evening like a beacon. She wore a bright red knitted scarf that wrapped around her petite frame snugly, the colors vibrant against the winter backdrop.

"Ishiki! There you are!" Bibian exclaimed, her warm smile evident as he approached. "This place looks magical! Have you seen the lights over the fountain? They're such a perfect blend of colors!"

"They really are," Ishiki agreed, scanning the area. The fountain sparkled under a magnificent display of lights—twinkling in various shades of blue, green, and yellow, showcasing the essence of a joyous holiday.

As they stood together, watching in awe, Akira approached, his tall figure almost hidden in a fluffy winter coat adorned with a sleek blazer. "I was getting worried you two might get lost in the magic of it all," he teased, his calm demeanor easing into a smile.

"Not a chance! We've been waiting for this!" Bibian chimed in, her voice buoyant and infectious.

"Have you tried any of the food booths yet? I smell delicious things all around!" Akira's eyes sparkled with intrigue.

"Not yet! Ishiki got us some sweet treats! We can scan the booths together later," Bibian replied, her excitement palpable.

Just then, Yuki bounded over, her vibrant pastel dress catching the eye of everyone around her. She exuded warmth as she clutched a small paper cup of steaming hot cocoa topped with whipped cream. "I just got the best hot cocoa! You all have to try it!" she urged, taking a sip and sighing with satisfaction.

"Sounds heavenly!" Ishiki said, noting the way her eyes lit up.

"But first, let's enjoy the lights!" Bibian suggested, her voice filled with glee. Without hesitation, she grabbed Ishiki's hand, leading them toward the heart of the illuminations. "Look at that over there!"

As they moved deeper into the park, they were met with an array of whimsical installations—sparkling reindeer, playful penguins, and even a dazzling train that glimmered like it was ready to take off toward the North Pole. Each display was adorned with lights that flickered to life with the touch of magic, casting enchanting shadows that danced on the snow.

"Isn't this incredible?" Akira marveled, adjusting his scarf. "It feels like we've stepped into a fairy tale!"

"And to think we almost skipped it for karaoke!" Yuki giggled, her laughter ringing clear among the twinkling lights.

Ishiki, with his backpack of treats growing heavier on his back, felt a swell of happiness as they strolled through the festival. The laughter, warmth, and festive spirit surrounding them made every step feel like stepping into a cherished memory. Each corner turned revealed something new—a new spectacle of color, a new sound of laughter, a moment where time seemed to stretch.

"I can't believe how many people came to enjoy it!" Ishiki noted, appreciating the vibrant community spirit pulsing through Nakamozu. Families huddled together, making snowmen, couples held hands while smiling at the installations, and children dashed around, their cheeks rosy from the cold and laughter spilling out too easily.

"Let's get a group photo with the giant Christmas tree!" Bibian suggested, her eyes sparkling with enthusiasm. They moved over to the beautifully adorned tree that towered over them, glimmering with thousands of lights and ornaments that sparkled like jewels.

Using her phone, Bibian positioned them in front of the tree, capturing their joyous smiles as Yuki playfully tugged on Akira's sleeve and Ishiki and Bibian made playful faces at the camera. The laughter echoed even louder as they gathered closer, summoning the spirit of anticipation for the festivities ahead.

"Ready? Smile! One, two, three—Christmas cheer!" Bibian shouted as the shutter clicked.

"Perfect! This will be our Christmas card!" Yuki exclaimed, her eyes reflecting the lights of the tree.

Moments later, they mingled through the park and approached various food stalls adorned with Christmas-themed decor. The aroma of grilled gourmet meats, sweet candied nuts, and baked goods wrapped around them, making Ishiki's stomach rumble in excitement.

"Let's split some snacks! I want to try everything!" Bibian urged, her eyes darting from stall to stall.

"As long as we get a little of everything, I'm in," Akira replied, his calm mannerisms continuing to contrast with the bubbling excitement around him.

They began to sample treats as they went, delighting in steamed buns filled with savory pork, crispy potato croquettes, and sweet sticky rice cakes drizzled with syrup. Each bite was a celebration of flavor, a new taste offering a glimpse into the local culinary traditions infused into the festive celebration.

"Do you all remember last year's festival when we ate too many dumplings?" Yuki laughed, recounting the memory of their overindulgence.

"Yes! We barely made it back after that!" Ishiki replied, chuckling as he recalled the evening. "But those dumplings were worth every moment!"

"And these treats are just as good, if not better!" Bibian declared, lifting her skewer triumphantly into the air.

As they feasted, they found a cozy wooden bench nestled between two glowing lanterns. The four of them settled down, enjoying both the lingering taste of food and the laughter rolled back and forth among the shimmering surroundings.

"I think we should make this our tradition—coming together every year to celebrate right here," Ishiki suggested, his voice sincere as he looked at each of his friends. "There's something magical about sharing this experience."

"I couldn't agree more," Yuki said, her eyes sparkling. "It captures everything we love: laughter, food, friendship, and the spirit of this season."

"I'm in! Friends forever, through every holiday!" Bibian cheered, her enthusiasm radiating warmth as they all raised their cups of cocoa, mirroring the spirit of the festive season.

Akira nodded, his expression thoughtful yet warm. "Each year will hold different memories, but the essence of togetherness remains the same."

With their hearts overflowing, they took a moment to absorb the ambiance, gazing at the colorful displays reflected in the snow. The night whispered promises of countless adventures ahead, their friendship growing stronger with every shared experience.

As the hours passed, the festive spirit swirled around them, casting a veil of enchantment that enveloped their hearts. The vibrant lights danced like fireflies illuminating the night, and the snowy landscape shimmered, bathed in warmth and joy.

As they lingered longer, Bibian suddenly exclaimed, "Oh! Let's take one more photo before it gets too late so we can freeze this moment in time!"

They gathered once more, squeezing tightly together as Bibian set the timer on her phone, giggling as they counted down. "Three… two… one—cheese!"

Click! The camera captured their beaming smiles; their eyes glistened with shared memories waiting to unfold.

As the night continued, they strolled through the festival, their hearts full of laughter and joy. They exchanged stories and hopes, plans for the future swirling like snowflakes around them. The world felt alive—a tapestry woven from the bonds of friendship, the essence of culture, and the celebration of love that had gathered them all together that night.

With every step, they looked forward to what tomorrow would bring, ready to embrace whatever adventures awaited them, yet grateful for this moment suspended between the shimmering lights and laughter—a night that sparkled with the magic of the season.

CHAPTER 16: A TASTE OF TAIWAN'S CHRISTMAS

The gentle flurry of snowflakes descended from the sky, blanketing Nakamozu in an ethereal landscape that glittered like a fairytale. Inside Ishiki Nakamura's cozy apartment, the warmth of friendship emanated through the air. It was Christmas morning, and the aroma of delicious Taiwanese delicacies wafted from the kitchen. Bibian Moon was busying herself with preparations, her long black hair tied up in a cheerful ponytail, an eye-catching holiday apron hugging her petite frame.

"Are you all ready for a taste of Taiwan's Christmas?" she called out gleefully, her cheeks flushed with excitement as she chopped fresh ingredients on the counter.

Ishiki stepped into the kitchen, the delightful smells pulling him closer. "I'm more than ready! What are we making today?" His expression mirrored the anticipation bubbling within him, eager to share in Bibian's vibrant culinary traditions.

"Today, we are preparing a special spread of Taiwanese holiday treats! We have pineapple cakes, sweet ginger soup, and of course, the ever-popular Taiwanese-style beef noodles!" Bibian responded, her voice a melody of cheer as she expertly stirred a pot simmering on the stove filled with fragrant broth.

"Wow, it all sounds incredible. I can almost taste it already!" Ishiki marvelled, leaning against the counter to get a better view of the bustling activity. His eyes lit up when he spotted a colorful array of ingredients lined up on the table, each one sparking memories of family gatherings filled with love and laughter.

Just then, the doorbell chimed, and Bibian's eyes sparkled with joy. "They're here! It must be Yuki and Akira!" she exclaimed, wiping her hands on her apron before bounding toward the door.

As Ishiki helped arrange the kitchen for their gathering, he felt grateful for the opportunity to delve deeper into Bibian's culture. The holiday was an invitation to not only savor the flavors of Taiwan but to embark on an emotional journey through stories and traditions that would bind them together even more closely.

"Hello!" Yuki Tanaka greeted as she entered, her face glowing with festive cheer. She was wrapped in a pastel blue coat, adorned with a cozy scarf featuring playful snowflakes. "Merry Christmas, everyone! I could smell something wonderful the moment I stepped onto the landing!"

"Merry Christmas, Yuki! Come on in! We've just begun to prepare some Taiwanese special dishes," Ishiki replied, pulling her into the warmth of the apartment.

A moment later, Akira Yamamoto walked in, dressed in smart casual attire with a stylish blazer layered over a simple shirt. "Hello, everyone! The holiday spirit is palpable in here!" he declared, a bright smile sweeping across his face.

"Just in time!" Bibian said, her voice bubbling with enthusiasm. "We're about to dive into the cooking. I'm so thrilled to show you all how we celebrate Christmas in Taiwan!"

As Yuki joined Bibian in the kitchen, Akira and Ishiki collected the gifts they brought with them—a range of artisanal snacks from the local Japanese market—and settled down in a cozy corner of the living room, preparing to share a festive moment together.

"Did you bring the Christmas cake you mentioned?" Akira inquired, curiosity gleaming in his eyes as he glimpsed the neatly wrapped package on the coffee table.

"I did! It's a matcha flavored cake with a twist. I can't wait for everyone to taste it later," Yuki replied, her excitement contagious.

With the decorations still twinkling around the apartment, Ishiki felt enveloped in warmth, a stark contrast to the cold winter outside. Bibian and Yuki moved seamlessly together, their laughter and collaboration filling the kitchen with an atmosphere colored by joy and creativity.

"Do you need any help?" Akira called out, leaning over to inspect the countertops filled with colorful ingredients.

"Actually, yes! Can you help me with the pineapple cakes?" Bibian replied while rolling out a smooth sheet of dough. "It's a bit finicky, but I know you both will do great!"

With enthusiasm, Akira and Yuki jumped into the mix, assisting Bibian in pinching and molding the petite cakes. They chatted excitedly about their week as the kitchen soon filled with delightful energy, punctuated by the sounds of laughter and light-hearted banter.

"Did I mention that these pineapple cakes are often given out as gifts during Lunar New Year as a symbol of good fortune?" Bibian explained while kneading the dough. "The sweetness inside reminds everyone of the fortune they hope to bring in the new year!"

"That's such a beautiful idea!" Ishiki exclaimed, impressed by the symbolism. "It's wonderful how food can embody such sentiment."

With the first batch of pineapple cakes baking in the oven, Bibian shifted her focus to the ginger soup simmering on the stove. "Next, we'll prepare the sweet ginger soup! It's often served during festive celebrations as a comfort food," she said, measuring out brown sugar and fresh ginger.

Yuki, captivated, leaned over the pot, inhaling the warm fragrances filling the room. "It smells so comforting and inviting! I can't wait for everyone to enjoy this," she mused, poised to taste.

Once all preparations were in motion, the air became a harmonious mixture of sweet and spicy scents, a culinary embrace wrapping around them like a cozy blanket. As the pineapple cakes baked to a golden hue, Bibian took a moment to reflect.

"You know, Christmas in Taiwan can feel different from what I've learned from you all about Japanese traditions. Celebrations often center around family gatherings, with food as the unifying element," she shared, her expression softening as she thought of home.

Ishiki nodded, his heart warming at her sentiment. "It's amazing how food helps create bonds and memories, no matter where we're from."

"Absolutely," Akira added thoughtfully. "In our culture, the holiday season is filled with moments of gratitude, connecting over meals and remembering the essence of family and friendship."

"Yes! Gathering around the table, sharing stories, and savoring flavors of home—it's truly special," Yuki chimed in, her eyes glimmering as she visualized her family table decorated with dishes lovingly prepared with tradition.

With the first batch of pineapple cakes fresh from the oven, Ishiki took a bite. His eyes widened in delight. "These are incredible! The crust is flaky, and the filling is just the right amount of sweet. Bibian, you've outdone yourself!"

As Bibian beamed with pride, they continued their culinary escapade, finishing the soup and laying out an arrangement of colorful dishes representing both Taiwanese and Japanese flavors. The table transformed into a vibrant display of inviting food, each item carrying a story of its own.

"Are you all ready for the final touch?" Bibian asked, her voice bubbling with excitement as she placed the last piece of the meal on the table. "Beef noodles— have any of you tried it before?"

"I haven't, but I've definitely heard about it," Ishiki said, his curiosity piqued.

As Bibian served the rich, savory broth over fresh noodles, she explained its significance. "In Taiwan, beef noodles are considered comfort food. They're a staple enjoyed during gatherings, especially during the winter months when warmth is needed the most. Each recipe can vary, reflecting personal tastes and memories attached to them."

"You're making me hungry just talking about it!" Akira chuckled, eyeing the steaming bowl eagerly as he inhaled the delicious aroma.

As they gathered around the table, the atmosphere brimmed with excitement, anticipation sitting at the forefront of their hearts. "This is what Christmas is all about! Uniting, learning, and filling our plates with culture," Bibian asserted, raising her chopsticks with enthusiasm.

"To food, friendship, and the spirit of togetherness!" Ishiki echoed, lifting his bowl high as laughter erupted around them.

As the group dug into the array of dishes, each bite was a revelation, the nuances of flavors weaving a tapestry of experiences that pulled them closer together. They exchanged stories about each component—reflecting on the memories attached and transforming their meal into an anthology of culinary exploration.

"I can't believe how sweet and spicy the ginger soup is! It's warming me right down to my bones," Yuki exclaimed, savoring every spoonful.

Bibian smiled, "It's one of my favorite holiday treats back home. It not only warms you up, but it's believed to also promote good health during the winter months!"

"I can see why it's a favorite—it's absolutely delicious!" Ishiki agreed, his bowl nearly empty.

As the meal continued, stories flowed effortlessly among them like the rich broth over the noodles, intertwining their shared holiday experiences. They laughed and reminisced about past Christmases, discussing the quirky traditions they each cherished.

"I love hearing about your traditions and perspectives from Taiwan!" Yuki said, her warm expression reflecting the joy in her heart. "It's inspired me to incorporate more of these flavors into my own celebrations."

"Definitely! Each cultural experience makes our gatherings richer by blending our stories and traditions," Akira added thoughtfully, absorbing the significance of their time spent together.

Once they finished their meal, the table bore witness to countless empty bowls and evidence of satisfied appetites. There was a moment of reflective silence as they leaned back in their chairs, basking in the warmth of friendship that surrounded them.

Afterward, Bibian rose to collect the dessert—a beautifully crafted matcha cake that Yuki had brought. With a flourish, she placed it in the center of the table.

"Now for a sweet finale! This matcha cake is special, filled with layers of celebration and bright flavors to honor our time together," Yuki said as she gifted each of her friends a slice.

With the first bites of dessert, wonder spread across their faces. "It's so rich and moist! The matcha flavor is vibrant yet delicate," Ishiki said, savoring the unique combination.

As they enjoyed the final touches of their meal, laughter and cheer filled the room, echoing around them as they reflected on the magic they had shared.

"This Christmas has been one of the most memorable days! Thank you for bringing your culture here, Bibian," Ishiki expressed warmly, his smile wide as he felt grateful for this unique gathering.

"Thank you all for embracing my traditions and allowing me to share this part of my culture with you!" Bibian replied, her heart swelling with happiness, "I hope you'll carry some of these flavors into your future celebrations!"

With hearts aglow and spirits high, they embraced the essence of friendship that transcended beyond cultural boundaries. The table, filled with remains of their delicious feast, also held stories of their shared journey—one that would continue to grow and evolve with each gathering.

As the Christmas lights twinkled around them, the friends basked in the warmth of their bond, knowing that this day was just the beginning of integrating their diverse cultures into their ever-evolving narrative—a tapestry of togetherness woven seamlessly through the flavors, laughter, and love that filled the air.

CHAPTER 17: CONFESSIONS OVER FRIED CHICKEN

The crisp winter air wrapped around Ishiki Nakamura as he stepped outside his apartment, heading toward the lively streets of Nakamozu. The snow had settled into a soft, white blanket on the sidewalks and rooftops, seemingly softening the world around him. Today, he was looking forward to a change in routine. After the whirlwind of festivities and cultural exploration over the last week, he and his friends had decided to indulge in a food adventure centered around something quintessentially Japanese: fried chicken.

Ishiki pulled his hoodie closer, feeling a surge of warmth from the anticipation of the day. By now, he was fully accustomed to Bibian's infectious energy and Yuki's exuberance, both of which created an atmosphere of excitement about any gathering. Today, they would be recreating a beloved tradition for many in Japan: enjoying fried chicken on Christmas, a habit that had grown over the years, evolving from a Western influence yet now firmly integrated into local culture.

As he arrived at Nakamozu Station, he spotted Bibian first, her sleek black hair framing her petite face, shining like an excited star against the white background. She was pacing near the entrance, her bright red coat contrasting with the winter palette.

"Ishiki! You made it!" she chirped, a gleeful smile lighting up her face. "I was just wondering if you'd gotten lost in this winter wonderland!"

"Not yet! I'd never miss the chance to hang out with you guys," Ishiki replied, chuckling as he reached her. "Are we ready for some fried chicken?"

"Absolutely! I've been dreaming about it all week!" Bibian exclaimed, grabbing his arm playfully and leading him towards their meeting spot for the day—the cozy fried chicken shop nestled a few blocks from the station.

"You know it's not just ordinary fried chicken, right?" Ishiki said, excitement bubbling in line with Bibian's enthusiasm. "This place is famous for its flavors and unique takes on the dish!"

"I can't wait! Let's see what they have!" Bibian replied, practically skipping down the sidewalk.

As they neared the shop, the golden sign shined invitingly through the snowy haze. The warmth emanating from the eatery was palpable, and the mouthwatering aroma of fried chicken wafted out, enveloping them like a cozy blanket. Just as they stepped inside, Yuki and Akira appeared in the doorway, both bundled up in stylish winter wear.

"There you are! Were we late?" Yuki queried, brushing snowflakes off her shoulder. Her cheeks were flushed from the cold and her infectious smile brightened the dim entryway.

"Not at all! But we're ready to eat!" Ishiki said with enthusiasm, gesturing for his friends to enter the bustling establishment.

Once inside, they were greeted by the chatter of fellow diners and the sizzle of frying chicken. They settled into a round table near the window, the warm light illuminating their eager faces as they browsed the menu filled with inventive takes on fried chicken—spicy Korean style, classic Japanese fried chicken, and even a seasonal miso-glazed version.

"Let's order a bit of everything!" Bibian exclaimed, her excitement contagious. "I want to try as many flavors as we can!"

"I'm in!" Yuki agreed, her eyes darting down the menu as she bit her lower lip in thought. "Let's not forget to order a side of coleslaw and kimchi; they add a nice touch!"

Akira nodded, a steady smile on his face. "And we need some drinks. How about iced tea or soda? It'll balance out the crispy chicken."

As they finalized their orders and shared laughter over the array of choices, Ishiki felt a sense of gratefulness wash over him. Moments like this—filled with food, laughter, and connection—carried with them the essence of their growing friendship, transcending cultural boundaries.

Minutes later, their meal arrived, steaming and perfectly golden. The tower of fried chicken was a sight to behold, accompanied by colorful sides radiating flavor and excitement. Their plates were filled with intricate creations—each piece promising to transport them on a culinary journey.

Bibian's eyes widened as she reached for the spicy chicken first. "This looks amazing!" she exclaimed, preparing to take her first bite. Her cheeks puffed out like a chipmunk, amplifying the joy radiating from her.

"Let's dig in!" Yuki encouraged, mirroring Bibian's energy as they each grabbed pieces of chicken, the crispy texture crackling delightfully beneath their fingers.

As they began to eat, the atmosphere erupted with laughter and playful banter. They exchanged thoughts on their favorite flavors—the spicy sweetness of the Korean-style chicken, the tender juiciness of the classic options, and the savory notes of the seasonal miso glaze. Each chicken piece sparked memories of food traditions and reminded them of their festive exploration leading up to this moment.

"This reminds me of my childhood," Akira said thoughtfully, his voice almost lost amidst the cheer. "We would always have fried chicken as part of our holiday celebrations, a blend of Western influence and Japanese celebration that felt special."

"I can relate to that!" Bibian chimed in, her lively spirit shining through as she dunked her chicken into a fragrant dipping sauce. "In Taiwan, we also have different variations of fried chicken, especially during family gatherings!"

"Food really does bring people together, regardless of where we're from," Ishiki mused, savoring a piece of the miso-glazed chicken. "I love hearing how our traditions overlap and differ. It makes every meal a discovery."

After a few moments of delicious silence as they focused on their food, Ishiki took a deep breath, looking from face to face. "Speaking of discoveries, I realized something during our Christmas celebration—about myself and our traditions. Sharing food means sharing stories, and I want to share something with you all."

He felt the warmth of his heart as the weight of his thoughts pressed gently on his mind. "I've often felt internal pressure to uphold traditions and to present everything perfectly. But with you all, I've learned that it's okay to embrace the imperfections. It's the shared laughter and moments that truly matter, not so much the organization behind everything."

"Ishiki," Yuki began softly, her warm gaze meeting his. "You've brought your own unique traditions into our gatherings. I see how much effort you put into making our time special, and it's appreciated."

"Yeah, and seeing you relax and enjoy the moment has been such a joy for us!" Bibian added, her cheerful nature reinforcing the bond they had formed. "It's about friendship, creating memories together, and whatever we end up eating!"

Akira smiled, resting his elbows on the table, his voice steady. "Every time we come together, we all learn something new. It's the melding of our cultures that creates this warm, rich tapestry of experiences. You're always open and willing to explore, Ishiki, and we appreciate your insights!"

The sincerity of their words enveloped Ishiki, solidifying their friendship even further. "I'm really grateful for each of you. You've made me see the beauty of blending our traditions and understanding one another."

Bibian clinked her drink against his, her eyes sparkling with determination. "Here's to more memories, more flavors, and continuing our journey together!"

Everyone echoed the sentiment, raising their drinks, eyes bright with promise. It wasn't just about the food—it was about the connection they forged, the stories shared, and the laughter that rang throughout their experiences.

As they finished the feast, the atmosphere around their table became filled with playful jabs and thoughts for the future. Yuki leaned in closer, a mischievous grin on her face. "Okay, confession time—what's everyone's guilty pleasure food? The kind of thing you'd eat alone?"

"Oh, I can definitely share mine!" Bibian exclaimed, wiggling with excitement. "Lately, I can't get enough of instant ramen. I know it's not gourmet, but it's so comforting! When I have a long day, that's my go-to."

"Instant ramen is a classic!" Akira acknowledged with a knowing nod. "For me, it's those small round rice balls with dried fish flakes. They remind me of home, and I indulge whenever I have late-night cravings."

Ishiki felt the warmth of camaraderie wrap around them again as he entered into the conversation. "You know, secretly, I adore those little snack cakes filled with sweet red bean paste. It's not something I'd usually share!"

Yuki laughed heartily. "Do you know what? I love Japanese convenience store sandwiches! They are so simple yet so good—especially the egg salad ones. I'd eat those every day if I could."

Laughter echoed throughout their table, each confession bringing the group closer as they reminisced over personal culinary secrets. The friendly banter, flavored with cultural delights, turned into a lively discussion, compelling them to share more than just favorite foods—somehow every morsel of conversation tasted richer, more fulfilling.

At last, with their plates cleared and their hearts full, Ishiki looked at each of them warmly, feeling an overwhelming sense of connection that transcended food.

"I can't imagine spending these winter days without you all," he said softly, glancing outside where fluffy snowflakes began falling again, blanketing their world with charm. "Thank you for being a part of this journey with me."

With the meal concluded, they decided to head back to the station, their stomachs full, but it was their spirits that truly overflowed. Stepping out into the chill of the evening, the festive lights twinkled above, illuminating their path home.

As they made their way back, Bibian took a moment to reflect on the day. "Next time, let's explore more about fried chicken around Japan! There are so many regional styles we've yet to taste!"

"I'm all in for that," Yuki grinned, warming her hands in her pockets. "And maybe we can have another cooking night soon! We should experiment with fried chicken recipes from our cultures!"

"Deal!" Akira added, a smile playing on his lips as they fell into step together. "Food adventures await us all year."

Walking side by side, each of them stepped a little lighter. They reveled not only in the flavors they had tasted today but in the unfurling narrative of their friendships—a mix of cultures, stories, and shared experiences that could only grow more colorful with time. The world outside may have been cold, but inside each of them, warmth bloomed, fueled by the bonds they formed over fried chicken, laughter, and heartwarming confessions that would surely become cherished memories for years to come.

CHAPTER 18: KARAOKE CONCERT PREPARATION

The festive season clung to Nakamozu like the lingering taste of a delicious meal, full of flavors and colors. After a whirlwind of food adventures and cultural exchanges, Ishiki Nakamura found himself buzzing with excitement as he prepared for the highly anticipated karaoke concert with his friends. This annual gathering was always a vibrant mix of laughter, music, and heartfelt performances, and this year felt particularly special as they aimed to blend various cultural influences into their repertoire.

Ishiki stood in his modest apartment, surrounded by the warm glow of twinkling fairy lights that he had strung along the windows. The room radiated warmth from both the simple decorations and the memories they represented—photos of past celebrations, each capturing a moment of joy that transcended cultures, laid scattered across the walls. Today, he felt like a conductor watching a symphony just before the first notes played, energizing the atmosphere.

As he set out snacks—a fusion of Japanese and Taiwanese treats—the sound of the doorbell pulled him from his reverie. He opened the door to find Bibian Moon standing there, her petite figure adorned in a bright, festive outfit that glimmered against the winter backdrop. Her smile was effervescent, lighting up the chilly air around her.

"Ishiki! I brought some special treats for our karaoke night!" she exclaimed, holding up a colorful assortment of Taiwanese pineapple cakes. "These are freshly made, and I really think everyone will love them!"

"They look amazing, Bibian! Thanks for bringing them," Ishiki said, his eyes twinkling at the sight of the vibrant confections. The sweet aroma wafted into the apartment and mingled delightfully with the scents from the dishes he had prepared.

Bibian stepped into the apartment, her cheeks rosy from the cold, radiating holiday energy as she began to arrange the pineapple cakes on a plate. "I can't wait for everyone to try them! It's a great way to start the evening. Plus, I have some ideas for my karaoke debut that I want to perfect over snacks and laughter!"

"Oh really? What are you planning to sing?" Ishiki asked, leaning against the counter, genuinely intrigued.

Bibian clasped her hands together, her eyes sparkling with glee. "I was thinking of mixing a traditional Taiwanese song with a Japanese pop hit! It'll show the blend of our cultures—we can even create a little medley together."

As they shared ideas, the world outside fell quiet beneath a new layer of snow, the soft flakes piling gently on rooftops. Each flake felt like another note in the symphony Ishiki hoped to create. Just then, another familiar face appeared at the door. It was Yuki Tanaka, her pastel scarf wrapping around her neck in a cozy embrace, bringing with her a wave of warmth.

"Hello! I came bearing the holiday spirit!" Yuki announced dramatically as she stepped into the room, her arms overflowing with colorful decorations. "I thought we could add some flair to our karaoke night! Streamers, balloons, and—" she held up an assortment of party hats, her eyes gleaming with excitement—"we can't forget these!"

"Yuki! That's perfect!" Ishiki exclaimed, appreciation flooding his tone. He loved how Yuki's optimism echoed through everything she did. "We need all the festive energy we can get!"

Bibian chuckled as Yuki began hanging the decorations throughout the apartment, transforming it into a lively scene reflecting their personalities. "Just wait until you see the outfits for tonight! It'll be the best concert ever!"

Ishiki couldn't help but feel the rush of anticipation as Akira Yamamoto arrived, his tall figure fitting perfectly into the jovial atmosphere. "What's all this commotion about?" he asked, a bemused grin on his face as he surveyed the preparations.

"We're getting ready for the karaoke extravaganza!" Ishiki replied. "Bibian and Yuki have some brilliant ideas for mixing our cultures in song."

Akira smiled, his warm demeanor continuing to put everyone at ease. "I'm ready to be dazzled by your performances. So, what's on the setlist?"

"Can't reveal everything just yet!" Bibian said playfully, her enthusiasm irresistible. "But expect a mix! I'll be performing a classic Taiwanese song and then jumping into a lively J-Pop number. Who knows? We might make an unforgettable fusion!"

They all gathered to finalize their song choices, the room buzzing with ideas and laughter. With time ticking away, the decision-making grew quickly competitive. Bibian's infectious energy inspired them to think outside the box, and soon they were brainstorming clever comparisons between their cultures through music.

"How about we also invite the audience to join in some sing-alongs?" Yuki suggested. "It'll be like a concert celebrating everyone's voices!"

"That's a great idea! We could create a fun segment during the concert where everyone can perform together!" Ishiki exclaimed. "It could be an encore of sorts!"

As the preparations flowed, Ishiki proudly surveyed the enthusiastic banter and collaborations taking shape. Each voice, energized and infused with the spirit of togetherness, added layers of warmth to his heart. The essence of karaoke—the radiant celebration of music bridging cultural gaps—had become their mission for the night.

As the evening approached, the group gathered the last of the decorations, laughter ringing through the walls of Ishiki's apartment. Bibian hung a vibrant banner overhead that declared "Karaoke Christmas"—a whimsical sign that perfectly captured their festive intent.

Once everything was set—decorations sparkling, snacks arranged, and spirits soaring—they huddled in a circle, excitement palpable in the air. "Now, let's go over the plans," Ishiki began, a sense of leadership threading his words as he took a breath, "Let's start with our solo performances. After that, we can transition into the group elements!"

"Perfect! I'll go first since I'm so excited—let me showcase how I marry both cultures!" Bibian declared, her determination lighting up the room.

"After Bibian, I'd love to do a soulful ballad that reflects my roots and also has a Japanese twist," Akira added, his usual calm demeanor transformed into passion.

After several moments of immensity and laughter, they divvied up the solos and group performances, their excitement growing as they envisioned the concert.

As the clock ticked closer to showtime, Bibian and Yuki suggested they all don festive outfits to enliven the spirits. They separated briefly to change into something bright and fun, and the apartment buzzed with anticipation as they prepared to dazzle not only with their voices but their vibrant appearances.

Ishiki quickly opted for a cozy red and green hoodie adorned with Christmas motifs while Bibian emerged dressed in a playful green dress with festive patterns. Yuki joined soon after, draped in a sparkling sweater, followed by Akira sporting a charming knit cap.

Once they reconvened, laughter echoed off the walls. "We look ready for a concert!" Yuki exclaimed, gleefully twirling in her outfit.

"Let's show each other how culture can blend seamlessly!" Bibian added, her face ablaze with excitement.

As the sun finally set, the room flooded with soft light from the stringed decorations. The atmosphere felt electric, a fusion of cultures hovering in the air, mirroring the melodies just waiting to escape.

"Okay, let's get started!" Ishiki said, his heart pumping with anticipation as he approached the microphone, a blend of nerves and excitement washing over him. He glanced back at his friends, their supportive smiles bolstering his confidence.

As the first notes of Bibian's chosen Taiwanese song filled the room, Ishiki felt as if he were on the edge of a thrilling adventure. Her voice soared through the apartment, vibrant and filled with emotional magic. They watched her, captivated by how she took them on a journey, each note brought to life by her infectious energy.

Once she finished, the room erupted into applause, resonating with the unmistakable aura of connection that only music could create. Ishiki's heart swelled with pride—it felt right to be sharing this moment with friends, reflecting their passionate blend of cultures through song.

Akira followed with his soulful ballad, captivating them with his unique interpretation. His voice melded storytelling with music, and the room fell into a hush, each person wrapped in the heartfelt beauty of the moment.

Yuki rounded out the solo segment with an upbeat number that invited everyone to hum along. Their laughter bounced off the walls, and the mixture of their cultures echoed proudly throughout the space.

As they transitioned into the ensemble segments, Bibian held everyone's attention, urging the audience—now consisting of their reflections in the brightly lit room—to join in. "Let's all sing a traditional Christmas carol together!" she said, brimming with enthusiasm.

With voices harmonizing in joyful unity, the spirit of the season spread through the air like confetti.

"I never knew blending cultures could be this much fun!" Ishiki shouted, grinning as they moved into a medley of both Taiwanese and Japanese songs intermingled with laughter and storytelling.

There were moments of joy bouncing off the walls, a cozy joy filling each note. They reached the crescendo of the concert with a final performance that combined their favorites—each style and melody a representation of their friendships.

Finally, as they wrapped up their singing and laughter, Bibian turned to each of them, her face radiating happiness. "This has been the best karaoke concert! Just look how we mingled our cultures together into something so beautiful!"

"Absolutely! We've made something transformative—from voices to flavors, everything just clicked!" Akira said, his voice filled with warmth as he glanced around the room, appreciating the effort they poured into crafting this experience together.

As their concert concluded, a lingering sense of fulfillment blended with friendship enveloped them, binding their cultures and allowing their unique stories to be united in unison. They closed the evening by sharing more snacks and discussing the beautiful experience of melding their traditions.

Ishiki looked around his apartment, seeing the decorations shimmering in the ambient light, the laughter still buzzing through the air. He felt grateful for the friendships they'd cultivated—these ties that crossed borders and brought them together in a blend of celebration and culture.

"Karaoke Christmas is officially a tradition!" Ishiki declared, his heart swelling with joy and gratitude as he took in his vibrant surroundings and cherished the company of his spirited friends. And as the night wore on, the laughter and music echoed; their melodies didn't vanish into the night, but instead resided firmly in the hearts they had come to share.

CHAPTER 19: A LESSON IN CELEBRATIONS

The snow had ceased its dance overnight, leaving a serene layer blanketing Nakamozu, creating a sense of magic as the city emerged from its winter silence. With the festive season still lingering in the air, Ishiki Nakamura felt a warmth within his heart as he gazed out his window. The memories of the recent karaoke concert mingled beautifully with the anticipation of spending the day with his friends—a mix of reflection and celebration felt fitting as they planned their next gathering.

The aroma of freshly brewed coffee filled his modest apartment as he prepared for the day ahead. Today was special—not just because it was another chance for cultural exploration, but because Ishiki wanted to dig deeper into the significance of celebrations within their varying backgrounds. He hoped to uncover the layers of meaning behind their traditions, which had recently blossomed into a shared tapestry of friendship.

As he sipped his coffee, he heard a lively knock at the door. Bibian Moon stood there, bundled in a vibrant, festive coat, her long black hair tumbling over her shoulders. "Good morning, Ishiki!" she chirped, holding up a colorful bag. "I brought something special for our day together—a mix of things from my family's holiday traditions!"

"Morning, Bibian! You're full of surprises!" Ishiki exclaimed, stepping aside to let her in. He noticed the brightness in her eyes; it mirrored the cheerfulness of the day.

"I thought we could start with a lesson in celebrations, focusing on how each of us interprets our traditions," Bibian proposed as she began unpacking her bag. Out came curious items—a small round cake, bright red envelopes, and various sweet treats that filled the air with a fragrant hint of nostalgia. "This is my family's version of a cake we make for New Year's, and these red envelopes are filled with little tokens —a way to spread luck and happiness."

Ishiki beamed, intrigued by the display. "Everything looks vibrant! I can't wait to learn more about it all. It's all tied to the celebrations, isn't it?"

Just then, the door opened again to reveal Yuki Tanaka, carrying her signature smile wrapped up in soft pastel colors. "Merry Christmas!" she greeted, stepping through the doorway, her cheeks aglow from the cold.

"Merry Christmas!" Bibian and Ishiki choroused together, lifting their hands in greeting.

Yuki placed a small bag on the counter, opening it with a flourish. "I brought some of my holiday favorites, including ingredients for traditional Christmas cake. I thought it would be a fun addition to our gathering as well."

"Perfect! We can mix things up, and at the same time, Yuki, you'll keep us grounded in your cooking traditions!" Bibian responded, her enthusiasm contagious.

Akira Yamamoto joined shortly after, his air of calm making him feel like the grounding force. "I almost felt like celebration was walking through with me when I saw all the decorations outside," he said, shaking off the cold as he entered. "What's the plan for today?"

"We're diving into cultural exploration!" Ishiki said, excitement bubbling in his tone. "Bibian has brought a beautiful selection of her family's traditions, and we'll blend it with Yuki's ideas about Japanese holiday cooking. Consider this a cross-cultural workshop."

"Sounds enlightening, I'm all in! I appreciate any chance to deepen my understanding of your traditions," Akira replied, his face lighting up with genuine interest.

With warm drinks in hand and a cozy atmosphere surrounding them, the four friends gathered around the kitchen table, each excited to share their rituals and the meanings behind them.

"Let's start with you, Bibian!" Ishiki said, leaning closer as he encouraged her to share her family's traditions.

"I would love to!" Bibian proclaimed, her excitement palpable. "In Taiwan, Lunar New Year is a significant festival, and it's often filled with joyous gatherings and family reunions. Food plays an essential role—like these treats I brought. The cake symbolizes longevity and the wish for a prosperous year ahead," she explained, pointing to the round confection.

"It's beautiful how food communicates such depth in these celebrations," Ishiki noted, captivated by her enthusiasm.

Bibian cleared a small space on the table to showcase the red envelopes. "These are called 'hongbao' in Mandarin. They're given to children or unmarried adults during the New Year celebrations, filled with money or small tokens for luck. It's thought to symbolize good fortune for the year ahead!"

"Lucky envelopes—what a delightful idea! It's like a tangible way of sharing blessings," Yuki commented, her eyes shimmering with wonder. "We have somewhat similar traditions where kids receive money during New Year celebrations in Japan, but they're often presented in decorative envelopes with auspicious imagery."

As they continued to explore the topic of celebrations, Ishiki shared about the significance of Christmas in Japan. "Even though we've integrated many Western customs, including fried chicken on Christmas, the underlying essence is family and connection. It's about welcoming others and sharing moments," he stated. "We often exchange gifts as well, but I prefer to focus on the time spent together—imagine how much more meaningful the exchange feels when you know the stories behind the gifts."

"Exactly! I love that every celebration serves as a bridge to connect us," Yuki added. "In Japan, Christmas cakes are often a symbol of the season. I can share how to bake one if you're interested!"

"Count me in! It sounds tasty!" Bibian chirped, already imagining the sweet confections in her mind.

As they gathered around the kitchen, Bibian took the lead and offered a practical demonstration of how to prepare her holiday cake. The friends engaged in the tasks together, their laughter mixing with the sweet scents of satiny frosting and the ingredients sprinkled around the countertop.

"Do you ever feel pressure to maintain the traditions?" Ishiki asked as Bibian cracked eggs into a mixing bowl, her hands moving with practiced grace. "I think with all the excitement of melding traditions, it's also easy to worry about presenting everything perfectly."

"Oh, absolutely!" Bibian admitted, pausing to reflect. "There's a certain expectation, but I think the joy comes from being open to flexibility. The most important part is not just the recipe, but the memories created while cooking together. When family and friends come together, that connection becomes the centerpiece of everything."

Yuki nodded, as she folded in the ingredients. "Yes! It seems the essence of every celebration, regardless of the culture, is about gathering, sharing stories, and creating memories. You can get so caught up in the food instead of what the occasion represents."

"You're right, Yuki. It's about balance. The past year has shown me that our traditions can evolve while still holding the core of what they signify," Akira chimed in, stirring the batter thoughtfully. "Embracing new things means inviting connections we never expected."

As they continued baking, Bibian shared stories of past New Years spent with her family during her childhood, describing how her relatives would gather around preparing the festive meals, the sound of laughter and storytelling filling the room.

"Those moments shaped my understanding of our traditions; I often think about how the flavors of home reflect the love and connection we share," she mused, her words laced with nostalgia.

Ishiki could sense the pride in her storytelling, and he felt compelled to share a story of his own. "My family observed a tradition of presenting a special rice cake during our New Year's celebrations, being symbolic of perseverance and prosperity. There's a confidence that arises in this act—a reminder of hope for the coming year."

"Oh, I love that!" Yuki exclaimed. "Every aspect of our food signifies a narrative that reminds us of how interconnected we truly are."

The afternoon swept by in a dance of flavors, stories, and laughter. Once the cakes were baked, they moved on to the icing, each friend eager to leave their mark on the creations. Ishiki watched as each frosting technique mirrored their personalities— Bibian's bold swirls, Yuki's delicate patterns, and Akira's meticulous approach.

"This is fantastic—look how beautiful they all are!" Ishiki said, feeling the warmth of friendship envelop them as they admired their handiwork.

As they set the cakes aside to cool, Bibian turned to Yuki. "Now, about your Christmas cake—how about a little friendly competition? We could have a cake decoration contest!"

"Oh, I love competitions!" Yuki grinned excitedly. "Let's see who can decorate the best cake with the themes of our cultures represented!"

Akira chuckled at the playful spirit. "Count me in as well. We could all take a piece of each cake home, doubling our memories and flavors!"

Excitement buzzed in the air as they gathered fresh supplies, determined to create edible masterpieces reflective of their cultures stitched into a rich celebration of friendship.

As they put their creativity to work, the small kitchen soon transformed into a canvas of colors, designs, and flavors. Each friend took the opportunity to build a cake that spoke to their own experiences, beliefs, and memories.

Bibian transformed her cake with bright decorations reflecting auspicious elements of her culture, while Yuki incorporated sweet pastel frosting reminiscent of Japanese sakura blossoms. Ishiki seized the chance to mix flavors, infusing a layer of matcha frosting with a hint of traditional elements.

Once their creations were complete, they all stepped back and admired their work, grinning widely at what each of them had produced.

"I think we should have a taste test to see how our decorations translate into flavor," Akira proposed, laughter cascading through the room as they each took a slice from their respective cakes.

Sampling their labor, the room erupted in reactions ranging from polished excitement to comedic exaggeration. The contest turned into a flavor-filled journey, sparking comparisons of taste that led them into deeper discussions about how each facet of their cultures brought forth different holiday experiences.

"Though these cakes seem diverse, my goodness, they are all delicious in their uniqueness! Just like our celebrations, every flavor contributes to the rich tapestry of experiences we share," Ishiki mused, savoring each bite.

Bibian nodded in agreement, takes of frosting lingering on her brush. "Food tells stories that weaves our lives together—it reminds us that even though cultures might differ, the spirit of celebration unites us."

As they sank into the comforting energy of laughter and spirited discussions that followed, Ishiki felt grateful for every moment spent together. More than just the culinary experience, he appreciated the insights they were exchanging regarding their cultural teachings and the importance of evolving traditions.

Wrapping up the day, they sat down with steaming cups of tea, content after a day filled with sweetness and reflection. Bibian lifted her cup toward her friends, "Cheers to all of our celebrations! May we carry these experiences and flavors into the future, inviting more moments like today."

"Cheers!" they said in unison, sipping together, their bond growing deep as they reflected on their friendship.

In that moment, the essence of cultural exploration intertwined perfectly with the joyous spirit of celebration. They had transformed individual traditions into a mosaic of shared experience, ready to embrace the ever-changing landscape of their lives and traditions.

As Ishiki looked around at the vibrant features surrounding him—laughter, delicious flavors, and the bonds they had formed—he felt a sense of hope and peace to carry into the new year, knowing that their collective journey had only just begun.

CHAPTER 20: EXCHANGE OF CULTURES

The soft chime of the bells at Nakamozu Station echoed through the crisp, late December air as Ishiki Nakamura stepped off the train, his heart light with the anticipation of the day ahead. A thin layer of snow covered the ground, glistening beneath the morning sun like powdered sugar. Today was not just another day; it was a day for connection, a celebration of the rich tapestry of cultures that had intertwined through the friendships he had cultivated over the past months.

He made his way to the cozy café just outside the station where he had arranged to meet his close friends: Bibian, Yuki, and Akira. Each of them brought a unique flavor to their gatherings, and today they had decided to explore another layer of cultural exchange. The first snow of the season had blanketed Nakamozu in a festive spirit, and they were eager to share not just food but also stories, traditions, and experiences.

As Ishiki entered the café, the warm air enveloped him, mingling with the aroma of freshly brewed coffee and sweet pastries. The interior buzzed with cheerful chatter, reminiscent of laughter that echoed in his heart. He spotted Bibian right away, seated at a corner table, her petite figure adorned in a vibrant red scarf, a cheerful splash of color against the wintry backdrop. Her long black hair was pulled back in a carefree ponytail, and her expressive eyes sparkled as she waved enthusiastically.

"Ishiki! You made it!" she beamed, her warmth igniting the cozy atmosphere around them. "I have so much to tell you about today! I'm so excited!"

"Good morning, Bibian!" Ishiki replied, returning her smile with one of his own as he settled into the seat opposite her. "What's on the agenda today?"

"I thought it would be fun for us to share our home-cooked meals from our cultures," she suggested, her excitement palpable. "I'll prepare a traditional Taiwanese dish, and I'd love for you to share something authentic from Japan!"

"That sounds wonderful! I could whip up some homemade ramen," Ishiki replied, already envisioning the preparation of the dish. "It's warming and hearty, perfect for this winter day!"

Just then, Yuki Tanaka and Akira Yamamoto entered the café, their cheeks flushed from the cold. Yuki was bundled in a pastel-colored coat, and her eyes sparkled with enthusiasm. Akira's reserved nature was evident, but even he held a gentle smile that brightened the room.

"Merry Christmas! Sorry we're a little late!" Yuki exclaimed, shaking off her coat and sliding into the seat beside Bibian. "We got caught up looking for ingredients for our dishes!"

"Hey, no worries at all. It's all part of the fun!" Ishiki replied as Akira took a seat next to him, nodding in agreement.

"What did you all decide to cook?" Akira asked, already impressed with their collaborative spirit.

"Bibian is making a Taiwanese delicacy, and I'm preparing homemade ramen," Ishiki explained, excitement bubbling in his tone.

Yuki clapped her hands in delight. "Perfect! I'll make a Japanese curry; it's comfort food at its finest. And I've got spice blends that will add some extra flavor!"

"I'm all in for that!" Akira chimed in, leaning forward with an eager expression. "I'm thinking of preparing a simple yet classic miso soup, a staple in Japanese cuisine that complements every meal. It's hearty and feels like a warm hug on a cold day."

"Curry, ramen, and miso soup! This is going to be a feast," Bibian declared, her eyes wide with enthusiasm. "And we should pair it with a Taiwanese dessert! How about I make some sweet red bean soup to finish?"

"Wow, that sounds amazing! I love how each dish reflects our backgrounds," Ishiki said, feeling grateful for the way their culinary exploration brought them closer.

As they mapped out their plans, Yuki's attention turned to the colorful decorations adorning the café's walls. "You know, our meal themes could intertwine with the holiday decorations. Each of our cultures has their unique celebrations—let's also share some traditions while we cook!"

"That's a great idea, Yuki!" Bibian replied with a bounce in her seat. "We can discuss the significance of each dish and how it connects to our holidays. Food truly acts as a narrative for our cultures."

All four friends began to envision the warm gathering that awaited them. They settled into a comfortable rhythm, exchanging ideas and ingredients that would soon mingle in warm pots and fragrant dishes, bringing forth a blend of their traditions.

After finishing their drinks and excited chatter, they headed to the local market, a vibrant hub of seasonal ingredients and culinary delights. The market was bustling with shoppers searching for festive treats—every stall filled with colors and scents that danced in the cold air. Ishiki felt a thrill run through him as they maneuvered through the excitement, each stall a testament to the season's bounty.

"Look at all these ingredients!" Yuki said, her eyes wide with wonder as she pointed to piles of fresh vegetables and spices.

"Look here, Bibian! These ingredients are essential for your sweet red bean soup!" Akira noted as he picked up a bag of adzuki beans. "You'll need these to create that delicious sweetness."

Bibian clapped her hands with glee. "Yes! Adzuki beans are crucial. We must find some sugar and coconut milk to complete the dish."

While the friends gathered the necessary components for their meals, they shared stories about their holiday traditions. Ishiki spoke fondly about osechi ryori, the various Japanese New Year foods served in ornate lacquered boxes, each element signifying good luck or prosperity.

"When I was a child, I would help my family prepare osechi, and we would often have fun decorating our dining table with seasonal decorations," Ishiki recounted, his face lighting up with nostalgia.

"That sounds amazing!" Bibian exclaimed. "In Taiwan, we celebrate Lunar New Year with the custom of 'reunion dinner,' where families come together to feast and celebrate. The food creates an atmosphere of abundance and togetherness. It's so wonderful to see how our cultures celebrate togetherness through festivals."

"I love how every dish has its own story," Yuki mused while picking up a bundle of colorful vegetables. "Japanese curry has its roots in the introduction of Western cuisine to Japan, yet we've infused it into our culture, making it distinctly ours."

As they continued shopping, they gathered memories along with their ingredients—different holiday narratives intertwining seamlessly with the flavors that would shape their meal. Laughing and joking, they rapidly filled their baskets until they were laden with everything they needed.

Once everything was packed up, the group made their way back to Ishiki's cozy apartment, where the kitchen would soon be buzzing with the energy of friendship and the joy of cooking together.

"Let's get started!" Ishiki announced as they entered his apartment, and the wonderful scent of his previous decorations greeted them with warmth. The atmosphere felt alive as they began to unpack the ingredients, soaring anticipation swirling in the air.

As each friend began to gather around, Bibian pointed to the stove. "How about I start on my sweet red bean soup while we cook everything else? It's a simple recipe that requires just some boiling and simmering—perfect to prepare ahead of time!"

"That sounds great! I'll start with the ramen broth," Ishiki agreed, excited to share his own culinary skills. "A rich, flavorful broth forms the backbone of everything."

While they busied themselves, Bibian prepared her ingredients, cracking jokes and laughter echoing off the walls. "Like I said, my family believes half the fun is in the cooking—especially when you have good friends and amazing ingredients!"

"I completely agree!" Yuki responded as she began chopping vegetables for her curry. "Cooking is all about the experience, not perfection!"

Meanwhile, as Ishiki began simmering the broth, Akira recounted stories of his childhood traditions surrounding New Year's celebrations, expressing how miso soup was often enjoyed as an essential part of the meal. "I remember my grandmother's voice, guiding me through the preparation of miso soup, explaining how each component contributed to our health and happiness."

"Just like how each ingredient enriches our meal today!" Bibian chimed in, stirring the sweet red bean soup gently. "It's interesting how food reveals stories of our past!"

As the hours flowed by, the kitchen filled with the aroma of simmering broth, fragrant spices, and sweet notes of red beans. Bit by bit, their dishes were brought to life, reflecting the essence of their cultures interwoven like an intricate fabric.

"Alright, everything is coming together," Yuki announced, as she stirred her bubbling curry, the vibrant colors of the vegetables dancing in the rich sauce.

Ishiki tasted the ramen broth, a blend of umami flavors caressing his taste buds. "Perfectly balanced! The flavors are coming out beautifully!"

With the kitchen abuzz, soon everything was ready—a steaming pot of ramen, a hearty curry, fragrant miso soup, and Bibian's sweet red bean soup, all adorned on the table—a rainbow of dishes that represented not just food, but a culture swap borne from friendship.

Before they dug in, Yuki paused, her eyes sparkling with curiosity. "Shall we discuss the meanings behind each dish? These stories will be part of our meal too!"

"Yes, let's share!" Bibian encouraged, her excitement bubbling over as they gathered around the table, plates piled high, hearts open to sharing their culinary narratives.

As they shared their thoughts, the temperature in the room almost seemed to rise. Eating together felt different than just filling their stomachs; they were embracing a blend of flavors and stories that expanded their understanding of one another.

"I love Japanese curry because it showcases the fusion between our history and the cuisines that have shaped us. It's comfort food that makes the cold winter feel a little warmer," Yuki explained, her smile glowing as she served the curry to each friend.

Bibian nodded, pouring her red bean soup into small bowls. "And this sweet red bean soup is a dish that symbolizes reunion and warmth in my family. We enjoy it during gatherings, reminding us of the sweeter moments we share."

"Ishiki's ramen is a blend of flavors that tells a story of patience, boiling down the essence of life through simple, nurturing ingredients," Akira said, offering Ishiki a proud smile.

Ishiki chuckled, slightly shy as he added, "And every bowl is meant to cultivate a sense of togetherness. When we share a bowl, we're sharing something so much more profound."

As they continued to share their stories, the world outside faded away. It wasn't about the meal itself; it was about how their varied backgrounds came together, enriching their lives.

After savoring every bite, Ishiki leaned back in his chair, a feeling of contentment wrapping around him like a warm blanket. "I can't believe how wonderful this meal has turned out. Not only is it delicious, but it carries pieces of us!"

Akira nodded, quietly taking in the atmosphere. "It's amazing how food serves as a bridge between cultures, enhancing our understanding of each other and creating connections that transcend language and borders."

"Every ingredient, every story unfurled before us, and now we'll carry them forward," Bibian said, her cheerful spirit lighting up the room. "This is what being friends is about—sharing, learning, and embracing our differences!"

With their hearts full and laughter echoing, they began to clear up the table, engaging in casual banter as they cleaned the kitchen together. Each laugh was a reminder of the warmth of this exchange.

"I'll never look at food the same way again," Yuki said, wiping down the counter. "It truly weaves our narratives together beautifully."

"Agreed! To our next cultural exchange!" Bibian chimed in, her enthusiasm uncontainable.

As the evening wore on, they gathered back together, a lingering sense of satisfaction threading between them. With the day behind them, it felt like they had not only shared a meal but had also shared a part of themselves with one another.

Ishiki realized, in that moment, that the true essence of food lay in the memories created and the bonds formed—each dish serving as an anchor grounding them to one another in a collective journey. The flavors of Taiwan, Japan, and their newfound friendships would forever flavor their lives, enriching their tapestry with every shared meal and cherished moment to come.

As they bid each other goodbye, the air was thick with a promise—an open door for future exchanges of culture, food, and cherished laughter, making their worlds just a little bigger, a little brighter, and a lot more connected.

CHAPTER 21: THE JOY OF TOGETHERNESS

The sun barely peeked over the horizon, struggling against the heavy blanket of clouds that had settled over Nakamozu. It was an unusually gray morning, but for Ishiki Nakamura, the day held a promise of warmth and connection. As he sipped his freshly brewed coffee in his cozy apartment, he reflected on the vibrant memories his friends had created over the past weeks, each moment blossoming from the fusion of their diverse cultures into one cohesive experience.

Today, they would gather once more, not just to share a meal or indulge in karaoke but to celebrate the profound joy found in togetherness. The air was thick with the scents of leftover spices and sweet treats from their last gathering—a delightful reminder of the richness that food and friendship brought to their lives.

As Ishiki set about preparing his living space for the day's event, he meticulously arranged the table, placing a vibrant centerpiece of flowers alongside festive decorations that still clung to the walls. This time, he decided to create a fusion-inspired brunch featuring elements from Japanese and Taiwanese cuisines. Fluffy pancakes, served with matcha-infused syrup and topped with fresh mango slices, would combine the best of both worlds.

Just as he placed the last decorative piece, the door swung open, and Bibian Moon darted in, a splash of color against the monochrome morning. She carried a basket overflowing with assorted fruits and pastries, her energy lighting up the room like a burst of sunshine.

"Ishiki! I brought dessert!" she exclaimed, her eyes dancing with excitement. Among the offerings was a beautifully crafted Taiwanese pineapple cake, its golden crust promising sweetness and joy.

"Bibian! This looks amazing," Ishiki replied, taking the cake from her gentle hands. "It's perfect! We can share it as a centerpiece for our brunch."

"I thought we could even give a little backstory about it while we eat," she suggested as they moved into the kitchen together, the inviting aroma of coffee mingling with the scent of the pastries. "I've always believed these cakes symbolize warmth and good fortune, don't you agree?"

"Absolutely! Every dish we share brings layers of meaning, not just taste," he replied, stirring the syrup while reflecting on how impactful each gathering had been; it wasn't merely about the food, but the stories behind them.

The doorbell chimed once more, and Yuki Tanaka entered briskly. She was bundled in a pastel coat that seemed cheerful despite the dull weather outside. Her blond hair fell gracefully around her shoulders, and like Bibian, she came bearing gifts—this time, a bundle of freshly made Japanese dorayaki, pancakes filled with sweet red bean paste.

"Morning, everyone! I had to bring something for us to enjoy together!" she said, setting the dorayaki on the counter with pride. "I figured they'd pair perfectly with your pancakes, Ishiki. How are we celebrating today?"

"I was just telling Bibian about the significance of each dish, and how we can share our stories alongside the flavors," Ishiki explained, joy bubbling up as he poured out the pancakes onto the griddle, the sound of sizzling batter providing a satisfying backdrop to their chatter.

"That sounds wonderful," Yuki said, grabbing a spatula to help him. "Let's make sure we each contribute our stories while we feast. I can't wait to hear more about the traditions around your pineapple cakes!"

Moments later, Akira Yamamoto arrived, a hint of the fluffy snow beginning to melt off his shoulders. "Good morning! Sorry I'm a little late; the roads were surprisingly slick," he said, shaking off the chill as he entered. "I've brought something special to add to the brunch!" He unveiled a carefully wrapped box—inside, a selection of Japanese New Year's osechi ryori, beautifully arranged in bento-style.

"Akira, this is incredible!" Ishiki gushed, astounded by the effort his friend had put into the presentation. "You're really going all out this time, huh?"

"Just wanted to contribute something that represents my family's traditions," Akira replied, his calm demeanor emanating a quiet pleasure. "Each item has special significance, and I think they'll complement the brunch beautifully!"

As they gathered around the kitchen island, the warmth radiating from their laughter infused the room, a cozy cocoon wrapping around them as they prepared for the day ahead. Bibian, with her infectious spirit, took the lead. "Let's each take a turn explaining the dish we brought! I'll start."

Gathered around the delicately arranged food, Bibian picked up the pineapple cake. "This cake is special for many reasons. In Taiwanese culture, some people offer it during their New Year celebrations, hoping for good fortune. It symbolizes prosperity and welcomes life's blessings for the year ahead. For me, it reminds me of home—of family gatherings and the laughter we shared."

Yuki leaned in, her eyes sparkling. "That sounds beautiful, Bibian. My dorayaki does a similar job! It's a favorite from my childhood, often enjoyed at festivals or when I'd visit shrines, especially during New Year's. They symbolize joy and sharing; what better way to bring happiness to special occasions than through something sweet?"

Bibian smiled warmly at her. "That's lovely! Food truly can unite us. Akira, what do you have?"

Flashing a gentle smile, Akira gestured at the osechi. "Each compartment holds its own meaning in Japanese tradition. For instance, the black soybeans symbolize health, while the kamaboko, or fish cake, represents celebration and completeness. Preparing osechi is a labor of love for many family members; it's a bond that holds us together over generations, much like what we're doing today."

Ishiki felt the room swell with a deep sense of connection as he listened to his friends' stories. Each dish was not merely food; it was a thread woven through the fabric of their lives, a testament to the moments that shaped them.

"Well, I contribute pancakes," he joked, bringing everyone's attention to his creation. "But these aren't just any pancakes! They symbolize warmth and comfort. I grew up enjoying pancakes topped with seasonal fruits on lazy Sunday mornings. Sharing them here, with you all, embodies the togetherness that I cherish."

With their stories flowing freely, the brunch soon took on an atmosphere of celebration. They dug into the delicious spread, relishing each dish and allowing their tastes to mingle along with their stories. The flavors traveled across borders, each bite a fusion of histories shared around the table.

As they laughed over bites of dorayaki, sweet pineapple cake, and fluffy pancakes, the morning unfolded into an afternoon filled with rich conversations about their individual traditions. They learned about how Bibian's family welcomed the new year and the significance of rituals in her culture, while Yuki talked about her own experiences with Japanese traditional celebrations, including the mesmerizing lantern festivals.

Akira shared anecdotes about family gatherings, revealing how certain dishes were cooked for extensive periods, as the journey prepared them for New Year's celebrations.

"Every dish has a purpose, a message," he said thoughtfully, his deep eyes reflecting their vibrant conversations. "It's about nurturing not just the body but the spirit too."

Ishiki interjected, excitedly. "And the best part is, no matter where we come from, the essence of celebrating togetherness knows no bounds. It's not just our meals that connect us—it's the heart behind every tradition and each person around the table."

Bibian raised her glass of sparkling tea, "To us! To our joy of togetherness, to sharing traditions, and to the memories we continue to create together!"

"To us!" they cheered, their voices tinged with laughter, their hearts swelling with unity—a simple moment of recognition that transformed into a sparkle of celebration.

As the brunch began to wind down, the clouds outside slowly began to part, rays of sunlight breaking through, illuminating the intimate setting. The ambience shifted, the dreary morning now filled with joy and warmth, just as their gathering had infused each dish with personal anecdotes.

"I don't want this to end," Bibian said with a content sigh, her head propped on her hand as she surveyed the table filled with remnants of their meal. "Every time we come together, I feel a little more at home."

Yuki smiled, her voice tinged with wistfulness. "It's so true. We're creating traditions of our own, right? And inspiring each other along the way."

Akira nodded in agreement. "These moments matter. They're what we'll carry forward into the future—it's the continuity of culture through friendship."

"We should make this a regular thing," Ishiki suggested, excitement bubbling in his chest. "There are countless ways we can intertwine our culinary traditions, and now that we're discovering each other's backgrounds more deeply, who's to say we can't celebrate every season together?"

"Absolutely! Each season presents an opportunity for us to explore something new," Bibian said. "Let's keep this rhythm going; I'll even bring dishes from Taiwan and blend them into celebrations here."

Upon hearing this, Yuki perked up. "What if we made seasonal-themed events? Think of all the flavors and celebrations we could explore! We can learn about festivals from each culture and intertwine our traditions."

"Or perhaps we can explore different themes, creating a cultural calendar of sorts!" Ishiki offered, his enthusiasm infectious. "The fun really does lie in the journey."

Excitement filled the room as they brainstormed potential themes—Cherry Blossom Festivals, Lantern Festivals, and Lunar New Year events floated around, each accompanied by stories and rich traditions.

It was in that moment of shared brilliance that they discovered the beauty of their bonds, embedded within their laughter, culture, culinary exploration, and the joys of simply being together. Each gathering would serve to cultivate not just food but friendships, pouring love and warmth into the ability to stay connected.

As they commenced tidying up, the soft rays of sunlight poured through the window, casting delicate shadows, illuminating the scene with a touch of magic. The warm atmosphere that had filled the air embraced them in a gentle hush; the din of the world outside faded away, marking a moment frozen in time.

With the brunch coming to an end, Ishiki stood at the window, gazing out to witness a soft transformation—the snowy scene glistening, kissed by the emerging sunlight, allowing him to reflect on a profound realization.

Friendship had blossomed beyond borders, celebrating connections woven through shared experiences of culture and kindness. And as they all locked eyes, Ishiki understood that they had created something extraordinary together: a friendship grounded in love, laughter, and the joy of togetherness that would resonate long into the future.

The day would soon lead into evening lights, but for now, it remained a delightful space of unity—a testament to the simple yet powerful truth that everything tasted better shared.

CHAPTER 22: A NIGHT AT THE KARAOKE BOX

The streetlights flickered to life as the sun dipped below the horizon, casting a warm glow over Nakamozu Station. The air was crisp with the promise of winter, and Ishiki Nakamura felt a surge of excitement bubbling within him. Tonight was the night they had all been waiting for—a gathering at their favorite cozy karaoke box, where they would blend their voices and cultures into a harmonious celebration.

Ishiki made his way down the bustling street, anticipation swelling in his chest as he approached the neon-lit entrance of the karaoke establishment. It was modestly decorated, yet the allure of colorful lights spilling from the windows invited laughter from within. He stepped inside, greeted instantly by the familiar sounds of cheerful voices and the electrifying buzz of music. It felt like stepping into a realm where worries melted away, and the joy of singing overpowered all else.

He had arrived a little early, which gave him a moment to take in the atmosphere. The rooms were bustling with groups of friends and families, some cheering for solo singers, while others sang along to their favorite tracks. The friendly staff, adorned in vibrant shirts, navigated the crowd with cheerful efficiency, serving drinks and snack offerings.

"Ishiki!" a familiar voice pierced through the music, and he turned to see Bibian Moon bounding towards him, her vibrant energy lighting up the room. Tonight, she wore a bright yellow dress that seemed to echo her joyful spirit—its fluttering fabric adding an extra layer of charisma as she approached.

"Bibian! You're here!" Ishiki replied, his smile broadening. "You look fantastic!"

"Thanks! I'm ready to sing our hearts out tonight!" she said, her eyes sparkling with enthusiasm. "Have you decided what song you'll start with?"

"Something classic," Ishiki mused, mentally browsing through the myriad of songs that streamed through his mind. "I'm thinking maybe 'Haru no Uta'—it's a beautiful Japanese ballad that I always enjoyed singing."

"Great choice! But promise me you'll sing something upbeat later on! We have a whole night ahead!" she replied, her excitement infectious.

Their conversation was interrupted as Yuki Tanaka swept in, her presence as charming as ever, wrapped in a pastel coat with a matching scarf. "Sorry I'm late! I got caught up at a bakery picking up dessert for the evening," she explained, showcasing a box of adorable, decorative cupcakes adorned with tiny edible snowflakes.

"Yuki! You brought dessert? You're the best!" Bibian exclaimed, her voice chiming like a joyous bell.

"I figured we'd need something sweet to complement our karaoke session," Yuki said, her cheeks flushed from the cold as she set the box down at a nearby table. "Did you two pick your songs yet?"

Just then, Akira Yamamoto entered the karaoke box, brushing off the last bits of snow from his coat. "I hope I'm not too late! Did I miss anything exciting?" he inquired, a smile lighting up his face as he approached.

"Nope, just getting started!" Ishiki replied, grinning as he gestured towards the stage area. "We were just talking about our song choices when you walked in. Bibian is ready to bring the house down tonight!"

"Ah, the pressure is on!" Bibian laughed, her playfulness shining through. "We should all kick things off together, maybe with a group song! What do you think?"

"I love that idea! How about 'Let It Go'?" suggested Yuki, bright eyes sparkling at the thought.

"Perfect! Everyone knows it!" Akira agreed, and soon they found a quiet moment to select the song on the karaoke machine, the screen glowing like a portal to a magical world.

The anticipation in the air was palpable as they gathered around the microphone, laughter spilling over as they navigated through the beginning notes of the song. As the familiar melody erupted into the room, each of them held the microphone with excitement, their voices harmonizing together, creating a tapestry of sound that enveloped the intimate space.

Bibian, with her vibrant energy, led the way, her voice strong and full of life, while Ishiki complemented her with his mellow tone. Yuki chimed in, her pitch perfect, while Akira's calm resonance added depth. The performance was a delightful mix of personalities—a fun representation of their friendship.

As the song concluded, the room erupted with applause from their friends in nearby karaoke booths. They took a breath, eyes sparkling with laughter and joy. Bibian jumped up and down, her delight contagious. "That was amazing! We should record that for posterity."

Feeling exhilarated, Ishiki grinned at his friends. "What should we sing next?"

"How about I introduce you all to some Taiwanese pop? I've got 'Little Lucky Star' lined up!" Bibian suggested, fumbling through the song list as she fluttered with excitement.

"I'm in!" Yuki replied instantly, nodding enthusiastically. "Let's showcase the diversity we have in our musical tastes."

As they took turns singing their respective favorites, the room transformed into a vibrant tapestry of cultural exchange. Bibian's choice of lively tunes infused energy into the evening. Songs filled with tales of love, hope, and dreams transported them across time and space, each refrain echoing their unique backgrounds.

Akira took his turn with a soulful ballad that encapsulated the essence of longing and warmth that was ever-present within his heart. The soft, lilting notes brought an honesty that left the room mesmerized.

"I never thought I'd appreciate a ballad quite like that! You should sing more often!" Yuki exclaimed as she clapped her hands, her face beaming with pride.

With each song, they navigated through laughter, storytelling, and moments of vulnerability. Each lyric and melody brought forth snippets of their lives, creating new memories that they wove into the fabric of their friendship with each chorus.

"Alright, my turn!" Ishiki declared finally, selecting a more upbeat anime theme song that echoed through their childhoods. With a few jokes, particularly about the dynamics of singing high notes and attempting fancy dance moves, he seized the microphone confidently.

With Bibian and Yuki cheering him on, the enthusiasm heightened as the chorus rolled in. The laughter and playful camaraderie boosted the atmosphere, each friend urging him on with excitement—an invitation that pushed Ishiki beyond his typical shyness and into the fun.

As they continued to alternate songs, they exchanged stories about the cultural significance of each piece, sharing how music had influenced various phases of their lives. Yuki spoke of her childhood memories tied to Japanese pop songs, while Akira detailed moments spent with family listening to traditional melodies that brought his ancestors' tales to life.

"Every song is like a bridge to our history," he remarked thoughtfully. "They shape our experiences and values. I love how we can connect like this, despite our differences."

Bibian nodded, her expression reflective. "It's beautiful, and each song we sing leaves a little part of us behind—a way of sharing who we are."

As the night unfolded, the karaoke box remained filled with laughter and friendly competition, fueled by waves of delicious food and the ever-present joy that accompanied their singing. The energetic vibe swept through the small room, igniting warm feelings of conviviality that wrapped around them like a cozy blanket.

After a particularly hilarious rendition of a popular jingle that led to spontaneous dance moves, they decided to take a break and indulge in Yuki's cupcakes. The sweetness accompanied by peppermint tea provided a perfect contrast to the pulsating energy of karaoke.

"Let's do a song challenge! The next song has to be the most random one we can find!" Bibian suggested between mouthfuls of frosting-topped delight.

"Challenge accepted!" Akira laughed, scrolling through the karaoke song selection.

"I'll choose one in Mandarin!" Bibian added, determined to share more of her culture through song.

Much more than just a traditional karaoke night, this was a cultural exchange forged by flavors and melodies, each lyric echoing their journeys, their friendships blossoming through shared laughter.

As the evening continued, they transitioned into singing holiday-themed songs—embracing the spirit of Christmas with their own cultural twist. Though their backgrounds varied, they found harmony in carols and jingles, interchanging languages and celebrating a fundamental joy.

At one point, the room was filled with the melody of "Silent Night" sung in both Japanese and English. The blending of languages felt magical, creating an ambiance rich and warm, reminiscent of the gatherings they had shared over the holiday season.

"Let's wrap up the night with a banger!" Bibian said exuberantly, searching for an upbeat finale. "Who's ready for the ultimate karaoke anthem?"

The remaining energy buzzed as they deliberated on the final song. "How about something nostalgic?" Akira suggested.

With a few votes cast, they landed on the iconic "We Are the Champions." Ishiki felt a surge of inspiration as they nailed the chorus together, voices ringing in unison—every note underscored by laughter and a true sense of belonging.

As they finished the song, a great cheer erupted from their karaoke room, resonating throughout the small establishment. They basked in the glow of their shared joy, heightened by the electric atmosphere and the bonds they had cultivated.

The friends took a moment to catch their breath, looking at one another with glistening eyes of camaraderie and connection. It was a moment of reflection—time to appreciate how far they had come individually and as a group.

"Can you believe we sang all this together?" Ishiki mused, blissfully aware of how memorable this night would become. "I think we've created something special tonight. These songs will always remind us of our connection."

Bibian grinned widely, her eyes gleaming with happiness. "This will go down in history as one of our finest nights!"

"Agreed! We need to do this again soon," Yuki replied, her heart swelling with warmth. "There's so much richness we can explore and so many more songs to sing!"

Akira nodded, allowing a smile to spread across his face. "New traditions await, and I look forward to sharing more cultural moments like this."

As they prepared to leave, the warmth of their friendship enveloped them, a beautiful reminder of the night they had created together. The karaoke box was now a special memory etched in their hearts—a gathering place not only for music but for the intertwining of their cultures, a celebration of the essence of togetherness in each note sung and each laugh shared.

As they stepped out into the cool night air, the winter sky filled with stars, they walked home together, their smiles lingering as they talked about future plans. The beauty of their cultural exchange was woven through song, food, and laughter—unforgettable threads binding them tightly together, ready to face whatever lay ahead, side by side.

CHAPTER 23: HAPPY BIRTHDAY!—A CULTURAL TWIST

The sun shone brightly over Nakamozu Station, casting playful shadows on the bustling streets below. It was a festive day that felt special, imbued with warmth that seemed to promise new beginnings. Ishiki Nakamura stood at the entrance of his apartment, an excited flutter in his chest. Today wasn't just an ordinary day; it was a day of celebration. It was Bibian's birthday.

Preparations had rooted themselves deeply in Ishiki's mind over the last few days. He wanted to make this birthday a memorable one for his lively friend. As he set about arranging his modest yet cozy apartment, he carefully considered the nuances of different cultures. He had grown fond of how celebrations intertwined in Japan and Taiwan, and he planned on using that cultural blend to honor Bibian's special day.

"Alright, let's do this," he muttered to himself, glancing at the small stack of colorful decorations and the array of ingredients set out on the kitchen counter. With festive ribbons, balloons, and a cake that still needed decorating, Ishiki felt a thrilling rush of responsibility and excitement.

Just then, a bright knock interrupted him. He opened the door to find Akira Yamamoto standing there, dressed in a smart casual outfit, carrying a beautifully wrapped gift.

"Hey, Ishiki! Ready to make this a birthday she'll never forget?" Akira asked, his calm demeanor underlined by a hint of excitement.

"Definitely! Thanks for coming early. I wanted to surprise her with a mix of our cultures, and I could use an extra set of hands!" Ishiki replied, gesturing for Akira to come in.

"Do you have a plan?" Akira asked, setting the gift down carefully on the dining table.

"Absolutely! I'm going to make her a fusion-inspired birthday cake. I thought of combining traditional Japanese flavors, like matcha and adzuki beans, with a Taiwanese twist—maybe a pineapple filling? And then we can decorate it festively!" Ishiki explained, already feeling a sense of vision take shape.

"That sounds delicious and unique! I can help with the decorations once we get the cake baked," Akira replied, clearly on board with the endeavor.

"Perfect! Let's get started." With that, the two friends dove into a flurry of activity: measuring, mixing, and baking.

As the cake baked in the oven, the comforting aroma began filling Ishiki's apartment. The sound of laughter soon accompanied the sweet scent when Yuki Tanaka knocked on the door, her energy radiating through the air.

"Happy birthday, Bibian! Well, almost, anyway!" she exclaimed, momentarily breathless as she carried in a basket filled with colorful snacks and more decorations. "I brought some traditional Taiwanese snacks to add to the celebration! You'll love them."

"Yuki! You're a lifesaver!" Ishiki exclaimed, genuinely delighted.

Yuki beamed as she set the basket down. "I couldn't miss celebrating one of my best friends! By the way, do you have an idea for the party themes? I thought the combination of cultures could make for an exciting twist!"

"Oh yes! I was thinking we should have both Taiwanese and Japanese elements sprinkled throughout. We can incorporate traditional birthday customs from both cultures into the celebration," Ishiki responded, enthusiasm bubbling even more now that they were all working together.

"I love that!" Yuki grinned, her cheeks rising in delight. "I can help create some festive decorations, maybe with symbols from both cultures to hang around?"

Just then, the door swung open once more. A cheerful, energetic Bibian darted in, causing a gust of warmth and excited energy to fill the room.

"Surprise! I'm here!" she chirped, her laughter like a melody echoing around the apartment. "What are you all doing in here?"

"Happy early birthday, Bibian!" Akira, Yuki, and Ishiki chimed in unison, laughter intertwining with their well-wishing.

"Why are you all acting so secretive?" she asked playfully, her curiosity piqued.

"Let's just say we wanted to help make your birthday special. You have to trust us!" Ishiki said, a grin dancing across his face.

"Trust? Alright, I'll trust you... but I want to see what you're all up to!" she laughed, glancing around the apartment in search of clues revealing the surprise.

"Okay, first things first—how about we all get into the festive spirit? Let's decorate!" Yuki suggested, breaking the suspense.

The atmosphere quickly transformed into collaborative chaos. Ribbons were strung across the room, colorful confetti scattered, and thematic decorations came alive, blending the vibrancy of Taiwanese birthday traditions with the subtle elegance of Japanese aesthetics.

"Did you know that in Taiwan, they often celebrate with a giant birthday bun that brings good luck?" Bibian informed them as they worked. "It's shaped like a dragon or fish to symbolize abundance and is usually filled with various ingredients to represent prosperity."

"We have something similar with our cakes too, where decoration and flavor can signify good fortune!" Ishiki replied excitedly. "We can connect those themes into the cake we're baking for you."

The conversation flowed like the chatter of old friends, and soon, the kitchen was abuzz with tales of age-old birthday traditions. The cake was finally baked and well on its way to becoming a work of art, with layers of luscious vanilla infused with pineapple filling, complemented by the sweet whispers of matcha frosting.

Once decorated, Yuki added decorative slices of pineapple to give it a tropical flair, while Akira took the reins on positioning edible gold onto the cake, representing prosperity—a vital part of both cultural traditions.

"Just like our friendships, this cake embodies our connectedness, blending our backgrounds and flavors," Akira remarked, carefully handling the finishing touches with gentle precision.

"Exactly!" Ishiki said, his heart swelling as the cake took shape, a tangible symbol of friendship and cultural intertwining.

As they meticulously arranged the cake on the dining table, they paused to admire their work—a masterpiece proclaiming, "Happy Birthday Bibian!" in both Japanese and Mandarin, beautifully written with carefully crafted icing.

"Let's add some festive candles!" Yuki suggested, rummaging through the supplies they had gathered. As she unwrapped a beautiful set of candles adorned with pastel colors, she felt the anticipation radiate.

Finally, it was time for the moment they had worked towards tirelessly. With each friend holding their breath, Bibian stood in front of the table.

"Make a wish!" they chorused as candles flickered.

With her heart full of cherished memories and the scent of sweet cake wafting through the air, Bibian closed her eyes and made a wish that echoed the very spirit of their friendship.

When she opened her eyes and blew out the candles, cheers erupted, the warmth of the day wrapping around them like a joyous embrace.

"You guys... this is amazing! I feel so loved," Bibian said, with a big smile illuminating her face. "Thank you for taking the time to make my birthday so special. It's perfect!"

They celebrated, surrounded by laughter and warmth, feasting on delightful cake and sampling Yuki's Taiwanese snacks, each bite embodying stories—not just of food, but of friendship, unity, and cross-cultural experiences.

"Let's make a toast!" Ishiki raised his glass, beaming at his friends. "To friendship, to cultural exchange, and to you, Bibian! May this year be filled with joy, laughter, and even more adventures!"

As glasses clinked together, warmth enveloped the room. They each took turns sharing their wishes for Bibian, offering kind words and expressing their love for the joyous bonds they had cultivated with each other.

"I hope your dreams inspire you to explore!" Yuki said with a twinkly-eyed smile.

"You've brought so much joy into our lives," Akira said, genuine affection coating his every word. "May your next year be as vibrant as you are."

"Here's to many more birthdays with friends who feel like family!" Ishiki chimed in cheerfully.

With the echoes of their heartfelt toasts lingering in the air, they dove back into the festivities, laughter cascading through the walls like sweet music, weaving memories that would be held close to their hearts.

As the evening wore on, warm tales of shared experiences echoed around the room. A sense of belonging was palpable; they were more than friends now; they were a family bound by cultural exchange and cherished adventures. Each laugh and shared memory pulled them tighter into the intricate tapestry, knitting their experiences with joy.

Amidst the joyful festivities, Bibian looked around at her friends—her heart fuller than she could have imagined. She felt gratitude swell within her as she whispered to herself, "This is truly a birthday to remember."

In that harmony of laughter, friendship, and shared traditions, the celebration grew into a loving reflection of cultural delight, each moment stitched together into an affirmation of connection and unity that transcended borders.

As they all huddled together in the cozy apartment, the candles flickering softly in the evening light, Ishiki knew they had created something beautiful; a celebration that honored not just one person's birthday but the weaving of cultures together—the essence of togetherness and joy that they would cherish forever.